TESSA HADLEY

Tessa Hadley is the author of six highly praised novels, *Accidents in the Home*, which was longlisted for the Guardian First Book Award, *Everything Will Be All Right*, *The Master Bedroom*, *The London Train*, *Clever Girl* and *The Past*, and two collections of stories, *Sunstroke* and *Married Love*. She lives in London and is Professor of Creative Writing at Bath Spa University. Her stories appear regularly in the *New Yorker* and other magazines.

ALSO BY TESSA HADLEY

TESSA HADLEY

Sunstroke and Other Stories

VINTAGE

21
Vintage
20 Vauxhall Bridge Road,
London SW1V 2SA

Vintage is part of the Penguin Random House
group of companies whose addresses can be found at
global.penguinrandomhouse.com

Penguin
Random House
UK

'Sunstroke', 'Mother's Son', 'The Surrogate' and 'A Card Trick'
were originally published in the *New Yorker*; 'Buckets of Blood',
'The Enemy' and 'Matrilineal' in *Granta*; 'Phosphorescence'
in the *Guardian*, and 'Exchanges' in *You* magazine

First published in Vintage in 2008
First published in hardback by Jonathan Cape in 2007

penguin.co.uk/vintage

A CIP catalogue record for this book is available
from the British Library

ISBN 9780099499251

Printed and bound in Great Britain by Clays Ltd, Elcograf S.p.A.

Penguin Random House is committed to a sustainable future
for our business, our readers and our planet. This book is made
from Forest Stewardship Council® certified paper.

CONTENTS

For Dad and Tom

SUNSTROKE

The seafront really isn't the sea but the Bristol Channel: Wales is a blue line of hills on the other side. The district council has brought sand from elsewhere and built a complicated ugly system of sea walls and rock groynes to keep it in and make the beach more beachlike, but the locals say it'll be washed away at the first spring tide. Determined kids wade out a long way into soft brown silt to reach the tepid water, which barely has energy to gather itself into what you could call a wave. It's hard to believe that the same boys and girls who have PlayStations and the Internet still care to go paddling with shrimping nets in the rock pools left behind when the tide recedes, but they do, absorbed in it for hours as children might have been decades and generations ago.

It's a summer day with the same blue sky and unserious puffs of creamy cloud as on the postcards. The high street is festive with bunting and flowers; the toyshops have set out their metal baskets of buckets and spades and polythene flags; the cafés are doing good business selling cream teas and chips. There are a lot of people holidaying in Somerset this year. Pink-skinned in shorts and sunglasses, with troops of children, they buy locally made ice cream, they visit the steam railway kept open by enthusiasts, they change twenty-pound notes into piles of coins and lose them all in the machines in the amusement arcades. Not so long ago, these old seaside resorts seemed to have been passed over for ever, left to the elderly by people rushing to take their vacations abroad; but now some people aren't so keen to fly. These tourists are congratulating themselves: with this weather, who needs to go abroad, who wants to?

Across the road from the beach are the Jubilee Gardens (that's Victoria's Jubilee, not the recent one), where there's a putting green and even a bandstand, though today there's no band. Two young women have established a messy family camp of bags, cardigans, plastic water bottles, discarded children's tops, half in and half out of the dappled shade of some kind of ornamental tree that neither can identify – although both, lying back on the grass, have stared dreamily up into the delicate lattice of its twigs and leaves, stirring against the light with an effect like glinting water. The children (they have three each) wheel in and out around their mothers' centre, wanting drink, money, kisses, indignantly demanding justice. The women hardly interrupt their conversation to dole out what's needed, to open up their purses, issue stern ultimatums. They talk, sometimes across the heads of the youngest ones, curled up hot and heavy in their laps, sticky tears pressing crumples into their summer dresses. The baby dozes in her pushchair, and later lies on a blanket blinking up into the tree, responding with little jerks of her arms and legs to the shifting patterns of light.

It's easy to guess even from the outward appearance of these women and their assorted children that they're not staying at any of the guest houses in this resort town, and certainly not at the refurbished holiday camp further along the front. They don't look wealthy (the kids' clothes are hand-me-downs, the purses are worn, and the women frown into them), but they look, if it still means anything, bohemian. Rachel's curving calves and strong bare arms are defiantly untanned; her luxuriant, nearly black hair is pinned up untidily on her head. Janie, who went to art college, wears a short gauzy green dress with seventies-style pink paisley patterns. Her hair, which is light brown and dead straight, is cut in some style that Rachel deplores and admires: ragged, uneven lengths, as if it had been chopped off at random. They are both in their early thirties, at that piquant moment of change when the outward accidents of flesh are beginning to be sharpened from inside by character and experience.

They have come to town just for the day. Rachel and her husband Sam have a cottage inland, where they spend their holidays; Janie and her partner Vince are visiting. Rachel and Janie have been best friends since school. They did their degrees together in Brighton and shared a house. When Rachel moved back to Bristol, where they grew up (Sam was working for the BBC there), Janie went to look for work in London and stayed. They're not obviously alike: Rachel is impulsive and can sound bossy and loudly middle class; Janie's more wary and ironic. But they tell each other everything, almost everything. During the long months between visits, they talk for hours on the phone. Both of them have other friends, but it's not the same: there's no one else to whom they can unfold their inner lives with the same freedom.

The two have been talking intensely today, ever since they woke up. First, Rachel came into Janie's bedroom and sat on the bed in her pyjamas while Janie fed Lulu, and then they talked as they clambered on all fours to tidy the children's mattresses, laid out end to end in the attic. Hours ago, they got the children dressed and drove into town; this was supposedly to do some shopping and get the kids out of the house so that Sam could get on with his writing, but all along they had in mind exactly the treat they are enjoying now – this lazy, delicious, stolen afternoon doing nothing, escaped from the men, talking on and on about them. They dip into their purses extravagantly, and the children sense the possibility of largesse. The older boys race off to the toyshop to buy guns for themselves, windmills for the little ones.

In order to earn this day in the sunshine with their beautiful children running around them, how many toiling domesticated days haven't these young mothers put in? Both of them do a token amount of work outside the home – Janie does a few hours of art therapy with special-needs children, Rachel does a bit of copy-editing – but truly for years they have been, half involuntarily, absorbed into the warm vegetable soup of motherhood, which surprisingly resembles their own mothers' lives, thirty years ago. They don't know quite how this happened; before the children were born, their relationships had shown every sign of being modern ones, built around the equal importance of two careers and the sharing of housework.

Neither is exactly unhappy, but what has built up in them instead is a sense of surplus, of life unlived. Somewhere else, while they are absorbed in pushchairs and fish fingers and wiping bottoms, there must be another world of intense experiences for grown-ups. They feel as if, through their perpetual preoccupation with infantile things, they, too, have become infants; as if their adult selves were ripening and sweetening all in vain, wasted. You can see this sensual surplus in them. It glistens on their skin and in their eyes, like cream rising to the top of the milk (though neither of them is fat: Rachel is tall and muscular, Janie slight and boyish, only her breasts rounded because she's breastfeeding). They half know this about themselves, how visibly they exude their sexual readiness. They know that they make a picture, spread out there under the trees in their summer dresses, with their brood gambolling around them.

The children press home their opportunity and clamour for ice cream.

—Pretty please, Mummy, pretty please.

—It'll keep us happy for much longer. You won't have to worry about us.

The guns the boys have bought were made in Germany,

and, on the packages, inside the bright orange explosion where it says *Bang Bang* in English it also says *Toller Knall*, which is presumably the German equivalent. The children point the guns at one another's heads, shouting, *Toller Knall, Toller Knall*, then laugh delightedly at how unthreatening it sounds.

—You know I can't bear that, Rachel says. —I have a thing about guns pointing at heads.

—Mum, they're only plastic toys, Joshua explains patiently. —It would probably be more dangerous to poke him with my finger.

But the boys give way cheerfully and aim at imaginary rabbits in the grass instead, squinting along their sights.

—Sam actually encourages it, Rachel says sotto voce to Janie. —He wants to take Joshua to join a gun club. He came out with all this stuff about teaching him respect for weapons.

—But didn't he used to fulminate against the arms trade?

—Oh, probably at some point. But for me it's not his principles that are the problem: have you ever seen him trying to put up shelves? It's not Joshua I'm worried for. Sam shouldn't be allowed anywhere near a gun.

Melia, Janie's middle child (much more difficult than the charming boys), pretends to get upset about the rabbits and ends up bursting into real tears. Rachel sometimes wonders whether Melia wouldn't respond better to a little less under-standing, but she preserves a diplomatic silence while Janie comforts and negotiates. Rachel thinks that she has taken more naturally to motherhood than Janie has; Janie is dreamier and misses her solitude painfully.

—Maybe ice cream would be a good idea, Janie decides.

The children plant their coloured plastic windmills in the grass and run to queue at the yellow-and-white painted café. Rachel is telling Janie about a man, Kieran, a friend of Sam's in London, who she thinks she might have some sort of a thing going with. Janie knows Kieran, too, though not well.

—It's really nothing, it's probably nothing, Rachel says. —You'll think I'm making it all up. Only it's funny that he turned up one evening last month, while he was back in Bristol visiting his parents. I'm sure he knew that Sam was going to be out. I had Sukey and Dom in the bath, I had my sleeves rolled up, I was in my foulest old clothes, my hair was just pulled into this elastic band, I'm sure I hadn't brushed it since I got up in the morning.

—Maybe he goes for that, Janie says. —You know how some men have this idea of domesticated women that really turns them on – only the ones who aren't living with them, needless to say.

—Joshua answered the doorbell or I wouldn't have even bothered. And then I thought he'd just leave because Sam wasn't there, but he came into the bathroom and he helped me out with the kids and actually it was really nice – we just got on so well. He cleaned the bath out afterwards while I was reading to them; I didn't even realise that till later. Sam would never, ever think of cleaning out the bath unless I asked him to. I always thought Kieran was such a serious sort of intellectual – you know, only interested in talking about Habermas or Adorno or something. But we were joking away, and then he was telling me about his sister's children. Dom was splashing us with his plastic ducks, we were completely soaked, and I was so apologetic, only Kieran said he loved it. 'I love it,' he said. And then I thought afterwards, What was he trying to say? What exactly did he love? Only perhaps I'm taking it the wrong way.

Janie thinks that Rachel is dangerously susceptible to men; she thinks that her own sceptical suspicion of them makes her much shrewder in her assessments of their motivations and characters. Also, she doesn't know how Rachel can put up with Sam's moods. She has her own problems with Vince, but she would never allow anyone to domineer over her life the way Sam does over Rachel's, with his black looks and his silences and his stormings.

—I almost dialled Kieran's number the other night, Rachel says. —The week before we came to the cottage. I did dial it, but I put the phone down before it even rang. I pretended to myself that calling him was just a natural friendly thing to do. I was only going to complain to him – you know, make a funny story out of the sort of day I'd had. Perhaps I should have. And I was going to say that he should come and spend a few days with us in the country.

Janie is solicitous. She is feeding Lulu, the shadows of the tree's leaves flickering over her bared breast and the baby's head moving with its rhythmic sucking. —Don't get hurt, she says.

Rachel throws herself restlessly down on her back on the grass. —I should be so lucky, she says. —As if.

—I'd wait, Janie says, —for him to contact you.

Later in the afternoon, Rachel takes the children for a round on the putting green. They are hopelessly slow because there are so many of them and the little ones take so many shots to get the ball in the hole, even when Joshua and Tom cheat gallantly on their behalf. Melia throws down her iron, sulks, traipses after them, joins in again. By the time they are halfway around the green several groups of players are backed up behind them and Rachel takes a break to let them past. She runs over to where Janie is watching from beside the pushchair. She has had an idea. When they've finished on the green, why don't they buy sausages and chips at the café so they don't have to cook tonight? This liberation seems of a piece with the lovely day. The drudgery ahead – peeling potatoes, frying, feeding, washing up – lifts from the evening as lightly as a floating cloud. Why not? Life might be easy after all. Rachel phones Sam and Vince on her mobile to tell them to cook themselves something;

she has to walk off a little distance between the trees before she can get a decent signal.

When Rachel switches off the mobile and turns round, Janie thinks for a moment that Sam must have said something vile. Rachel's face is concentrated with surprise; she walks back across the grass as if she were looking carefully where to put her bare feet.

—You'll never guess, she says.

—What?

—Kieran's turned up.

—Oh, Rach.

—But I really never did phone him. I never asked him. He's been before, a couple of times. Apparently, he just turned up this afternoon. He knew we'd be at the cottage because Sam mentioned it. Sam's going to make them something with pasta.

—Are you glad?

—It feels like a sign: that this thing I've imagined must be real, it must be something.

—I suppose so.

—I truly thought I might just be making it up. But you said to wait for him to contact me and he has. Sort of. It feels serious.

In all the agitations of the putting, Rachel's hair has come partly out of its pins; long strands coil on her neck. She's statuesque, with waxy creamy skin, like a Reynolds portrait; she doesn't have the physical lightness or fluidity that suggests affairs, easy transitions between men, concealments. The boys are shouting from the green; it's time for them to take their turn again. She picks up her putting iron thoughtfully. Janie can feel excitement radiating out from her like heat.

Kieran's arrival could have been awkward for the men back at the cottage, because Kieran and Sam have been friends for years, since they were at Cambridge, whereas Sam only knows Vince because of Janie and thinks of him as a bit of a lightweight. All morning, while Sam was at work on the computer, he was uneasily suppressing an awareness of Vince at a loose end downstairs, strolling around the rooms, reading yesterday's paper, getting himself something to eat. Sam was irritated that the girls hadn't taken Vince with them when they went to town; and then that they were staying out so long.

However, Kieran has brought with him a big polythene packet of weed, which, as they set about rolling it up and smoking it, produces an immediate cheerful camaraderie. They sprawl in the plastic garden chairs in the sunshine, smoking and drinking cup after cup of tea. Sam is so relieved he doesn't have to make conversation with Vince all by himself that he becomes expansively friendly towards him. He always forgets what it is that Vince does for a living (usually he covers this up by talking about the contemporary novel: Sam had one published three years ago and is supposed to be working on the next). Tactfully now, he leads the conversation around to the kind of crossover electronic music he remembers Vince likes, and Vince tells them that he designed the lighting recently for a concert in the Queen Elizabeth Hall. Vince is eager to please. He is lean, with the wedge-narrow face of a well-bred collie, and his hair, bleached-pale silk, is cut to flop into his eyes. He has the kind of good looks that men don't mind imagining women like. Sam doesn't hold it against Vince that he himself is bulky-shouldered and putting on weight. His brown curls are thinning on top and he wears little gold-rimmed glasses; he fancies he looks a bit like middle-period Coleridge.

The peace of the afternoon seems deeper because of all the children's toys lying where they were dropped, the bikes beached on their sides, the swing hanging still. The cottage is tucked into the bottom of a crease worked deep between the rounded slopes of the hills; sheep are grazing in the field that rises so steeply behind them that you can almost touch their roof from the path that winds along its lower edge. In the wide bowlful of tender light the buzzards sail superbly, mewing and turning their pale undersides to the declining sun. Wrens are pecking the greenfly from Rachel's sweet-pea plants.

Kieran is telling the others about his grandfather who worked as a salesman for a company selling private telephone systems, mostly to the collieries; he did business in the West Country coalfield that's not far from the cottage, worked out and half forgotten now. The telephones they used down the mines were made of cast iron, he tells them; they weighed a hundredweight each. Kieran is shorter than the other two; he has a big distinctive head, with deep-hooded eyes whose glance mostly idles downward, and several days' growth of strong black beard. His body is indefinite, shapeless because it's wrapped as always in dark loose clothes, more layers than are necessary in this weather.

—He worked in North Wales, too, Kieran says, —putting in systems for the slate mines. Do you know that when the slate miners were dying of silicosis, average life expectancy thirty-five to forty, the local doctors wrote a paper blaming it on the stewed tea they drank?

Kieran always knows things; he trusts facts more than opinions. He talks with his usual concentration and exactitude, but something arouses in Sam the solicitude for his welfare that has been an element of their friendship from the beginning. Kieran's face is puffy and a nerve is jumping beside his right eye; he hunches over the rolling papers in a tension of fatigue that makes Sam worry that the job in cardiology at Barts is disillusioning, and that Kieran is beginning to brood over this second career, which was supposed to save his life from academic futility. He isn't telling his stories any more, about medical dilemmas or patients presenting extraordinary symptoms. In these stories, his work in medicine seemed to open up a whole world of meaning.

Rachel telephones the cottage to tell Sam that she and Janie are going to buy tea for the kids in town. He's relieved that she doesn't seem to mind Kieran's turning up. After another cup of tea and a share of the toke, Sam goes into the kitchen, opens the door of the fridge, and stands frowning perplexedly at what's inside, then begins with an air of bemusement, as if he's never done it before, to make the tomato sauce he's actually been able to cook for at least fifteen years. He rattles around in the kitchen drawers hunting for wooden spoons and the garlic press. Kieran in the garden opens a bottle of wine he brought. Vince turns out to know something about wine. Kieran doesn't; he just drinks it. He's the same with food: he only eats to fuel his system.

Vince was uncomfortable at first, alone with these two men who are a few years older than him and whose displays of cleverness he finds both irritating and intimidating. He reads, but he hasn't read any of the books they've read. (He knows that they studied literature, but as far as he can see they mostly talk about philosophy.) This morning, when Janie went out with Rachel and all the kids and Sam was writing upstairs, Vince wondered what point there was in his being here (wasn't the whole idea of the holiday that he was supposed to spend more time with the kids?), and he even contemplated driving back to London and coming down to pick them up at the weekend. He was just wasting days that he could be putting in at the studio. After a few smokes, though, his sociable nature has reasserted itself and he is enjoying everything. He's looking forward to the kids coming back; he really does want to spend more time with them.

When Sam goes into the kitchen to cook, Vince finds himself telling Kieran in great detail about the logistics of the lighting set-up he's arranging for a show at the Albany.

He is gratified by Kieran's questioning. He tells him about the concern in the industry over the decline in the quality of sound recording in television and documentary work, now that digital technology means that no one bothers to employ the old sound guys any more. The BECTU newsletter is full of laments for past standards. Kieran makes a much better listener than Sam, Vince thinks. Sam always wants to take over the conversation. Vince has tried to read Sam's novel but can't get past the second chapter. None of the characters ever have a thought that doesn't lead into dense thickets of historical and cultural association. There is no room left over for anything actually to happen.

When Janie and Rachel come through the gate into the garden, Kieran stands up at once from where the men (stoned, by the looks of it) are sprawled on garden chairs. There are plates on the table and a saucepan lying nearby on the grass. Both women see quite clearly that the moment they come into view, their arms full of children and shopping, Kieran is looking for Rachel, and that on his face when he sees her there is a moment's naked flash of feeling: of relief, perhaps, or desperation. He hurries forward to help them. In reaction to this glimpse of emotion, Rachel becomes queenly and remote, retreating into her role as homemaker, unpacking the shopping into the kitchen cupboards and the fridge, running hot water for the dirty pasta plates.

Soon after their arrival home, Sukey begins to droop. This isn't usual: she is a cheerful little girl with stout strong arms and legs and a mop of straw-textured fair hair. Now she whines and clings to Rachel and says that her head hurts. Her face is flushed and hot, and as soon as Rachel gets her settled on the sofa with her doggie and her blanket she throws up over everything.

—Too much sun. My fault, Rachel says, on her hands

and knees with a cloth and a bucket of disinfectant and water. Sukey lies languidly across Sam's lap, wrapped in a sheet and hanging on to a plastic bowl. —I should have insisted she wore her hat. I should have made them stay in the shade more.

—We needn't go to the pub, Sam says. —If you think we oughtn't.

There has been a plan for all the adults to go to the pub, which is ten minutes' walk down the road into the village, leaving Joshua and Tom in charge, with mobiles in case of emergency.

—The rest of you go, Rachel says. —I'm sure there's nothing to worry about. But I'm feeling quite tired. I fancy an early night. And I probably should just keep an eye on her.

Kieran drops on his haunches till he's at Sukey's level, he speaks to her gravely, sweetly; she yields herself, allows him to feel her forehead, pull back her eyelids and look into her pupils, take her pulse. His fingers, with their bitten yellow nails and curling black hairs, are dark and coarsely male against her pearl-pink skin. Rachel's eyes are fixed on Kieran's face, calmly enough.

He says to Sukey, —Mummy knows exactly what the matter is. I would trust her. Mummies usually know best. I don't think there's anything to worry about here.

And he smiles into Rachel's expectant open gaze.

Kieran doesn't smile very often. When he does, his face becomes quite jolly and ordinary. It's like a reprieve, as if a daunting problem had unexpectedly turned out to be easy.

—Why don't you see how she is in half an hour? he says. —If she goes off to sleep peacefully enough I don't see any reason why you shouldn't leave her. It would probably be good for you to get a break.

—Maybe, Rachel murmurs gratefully.

13

Sam thinks that if Kieran can get this out of being a doctor – this exchange of authority and submissive trust – then perhaps everything will be all right for him after all.

Upstairs, fifteen minutes later, Janie and Rachel are giving Dom and Melia a bath.

—Rach, why don't you go to the pub? I really don't mind staying in. Anyway, I'm worried in case Lulu doesn't sleep through. I can call you if Sukey's sick again.

—No, honestly. I'd rather not.

—I just thought, you know, if Kieran's only here for tonight.

Rachel hides her involuntary smile in Dom's frog-flannel. —There is something, isn't there? she whispers.

—God, yes, Janie whispers back. —The way he looked at you when we came in.

—I know.

—Then go to the pub.

—No. I don't think so. I'm not ready. I'm not ready for it yet.

Sukey doesn't throw up again; her temperature comes down. Rachel reads to her and then sits beside her bed until she is soundly asleep. All the other children are asleep, too, by this time, except Joshua and Tom, who are watching a DVD in the front room. Rachel goes downstairs and out into the garden. The light is draining imperceptibly out of the sky; the velvety plum colour of the copper beech is drinking up darkness. Yellow light from inside the house glitters on the stone flags of the patio. Through the French windows, the TV flickers behind the silhouetted heads of the boys intently watching.

Vince comes back from the pub for his fags. He stops to smoke one in the garden. She has one, too, although she doesn't usually, and they experience a rush of mutual friendliness. Vince thinks Rachel's a sweet woman, not his type but warm and nurturing. Rachel feels sorry for Vince – she thinks Janie gives him a hard time. He tells her that he's really enjoying himself (he's forgotten how he felt in the morning). He says that this place means a lot to him, that he and Janie really ought to try to move out of London. It isn't fair bringing kids up there; they need wide open spaces and contact with nature. Rachel listens to him indulgently, knowing that nothing will come of it, and that Vince would fade away with boredom in the country.

When he's gone, a clamour of rooks passes overhead. It's darker now. Moths come visiting Rachel's chive flowers and nicotiana in a pale blur of movement. A bat stirs the air with a beat of its leathery wings. There's a moment's impulse when she thinks she'll tell the boys that she's going to the pub after all, and that they have to listen for the babies. But she doesn't move, she stays planted there in the still air darting with invisible movement, washed in streams of incense from the balsam poplar.

On the way home from the pub, Janie and Kieran fall behind the others because she stops to listen when he says that he can hear an owl hunting. She is genuinely delighted when she hears it too. These two haven't spoken together much during the evening. Sam and Kieran were arguing about Iraq (it's typical of Kieran that he won't condemn the war, when everybody else does). She and Vince were having one of their talks, about how he's got to start being home more, to make space for her to get on with her art work. (Vince didn't point out tonight, not in so many words, that his work brings in money and hers doesn't.) Janie has never quite trusted Kieran; she's always thought that he was one of Sam's Cambridge types, too absorbed in himself, preoccupied with the game of jockeying for intellectual position. She wonders what he's up to with Rachel.

The stretch of road outside the pub is lit, but when they turn off to climb the hill to the cottage they are plunged into a darkness deep and complete and astonishing to these city folk, who are used to the perpetual urban orange seepage of light. They didn't think to bring a torch. Walking into that darkness, solid and prohibitive, feels as counter-intuitive as walking into a wall.

Janie falters. —I've no idea where I'm going, she says.

—Hold on to me, Kieran says, reaching out. —Though I've absolutely no idea, either.

—I suppose at least if we fall into anything we'll go together.

They can't see each other; she feels his hand come searching, and she clasps his upper arm, when she finds it, with both her hands. She remembers what he's wearing – a green shirt patterned with yellow motifs in some kind of slippery material – as if it were suddenly significant, although she's been looking at it without interest (if anything, with distaste) all evening. The slippery fabric slides under her fingers. His hand blunders against her bare arm under the cardigan she has slung across her shoulders.

They can hear the others' voices some way ahead. —OK, Janie? Vince calls.

—Fine!

—Fucking dark! Kieran shouts. —Fucking countryside!

—Navigate by the fucking stars! Sam shouts back.

Kieran and Janie have both drunk enough to be unsteady, hanging on to each other in the middle of the road without any visual clues to help them. They stagger and he grabs her and pulls her against him and then begins to kiss her face with a beery smoky garlicky mouth (the garlic was in the pasta, which she and Rachel didn't eat). He lands kisses randomly at first, on her ear, on the side of her nose. After a moment's surprise, she kisses him back, putting her hand up into his hair and finding his mouth with hers. It's a long time since she's properly kissed anyone but Vince; she's pleased that she seems to manage it suavely and skilfully. Then her head swims and they lose their balance and almost fall. He sets his feet apart on the road so he can support her; he puts an arm around behind her shoulders.

—Who are you? he says softly, so close she can taste his breath on her. —It's so dark it could be anyone.

She can smell the salty sourness of his hair, too, as if he didn't bother with shampoo. —I've no idea, she says. —Who are you? What just happened?

—Don't stop. Don't stop, please. His voice is urgent, pleading. He means it.

Janie thinks that this is what he meant, when he looked at Rachel in the afternoon: he was just desperate to lose himself like this. She will do just as well, for his need, as Rachel; and yet that's not insulting but exhilarating. She feels the same way: he will do for her, just as well. She doesn't stop. She starts again.

His mouth is hot and liquid. His lips feel swollen and thin-skinned; his beard growth is long enough to be sleek and not stubble-rough against her mouth and her wet cheek. She thinks of the many parties at Sam and Rachel's where she has stayed dumb while Kieran has spoken out eloquently on some subject; and now that same tongue of his is shyly tentative against hers, and hers is bolder. It's marvellously simplifying that there's no time for this to become anything more than a kiss. They have only this moment before they have to follow the others and go back inside the light.

Vince calls again. His voice sounds a long way off.

—We're listening to the owl, Kieran shouts back.

It makes a space between them. They draw slightly apart.

—Look what you've done, Janie says.

She couldn't have said this to his face, in the light.

—What have I done?

She finds his hand, presses it against her breasts, where

17

they have leaked soaked circles of milk on to her dress.
—I'm still feeding. I'm very full. Ready for the baby when
I get home. You made it come.

—I didn't know that happened, he says, not embarrassed,
in a voice of calm scientific interest.

When he says that, Janie intuits a warning; faintly, like a
note sounding far off in the hills. She has an instant's intimation of how she could, in a different life from the one she
has had so far, come to need this terribly and not be able to
get it: this calm impersonal interest of his, turned on her.

But for the time being it is Kieran who is desperate.

Rachel thinks that she's going to lie awake, absorbed in the
momentousness of her life today. She's thinking that she's
not going to go through with this thing with Kieran, not
now, not this time. But that doesn't spoil the euphoria that
comes from knowing that he wants her, knowing that he
has pursued her down here. It makes her feel as if there
were a glorious abundant tide of secret possibility flowing
around the world, enough for everyone. She feels that she
will be able now to dip into this tide and take her share
any time she chooses to.

Sam is lying flat, snoring with his mouth open, because
he's been drinking and smoking. She shoves him hard to
tell him to turn over, and then when she cuddles up against
his broad hot back she falls asleep almost at once.

Janie has brought Lulu into bed to feed her; Vince is reading
a computer magazine. Her treachery in relation to him
doesn't seem important yet. (Vaguely, she thinks he owes
her this.) If she imagines Rachel finding out what she's just
done with Kieran, after everything they talked about all
afternoon, she feels a sickish kind of unease. She doesn't
for one moment, though, believe that she ought to have
deflected Kieran's kiss, which opened this thrilling new

space in the night. A real adventure with a man mustn't be wasted. Everything is running away so fast; your deepest responsibility is to snatch at all the living you can.

And, anyway, she only kissed him.

Kieran asked if he could call her and she said she didn't know yet, but as the baby sucks she feels herself hollowed out from her old life, empty and hungry, filled up with an excited wanting as painful and bloating as wind.

Rachel has made up the sofa bed with sheets and a duvet for Kieran. She kept worriedly sniffing it and saying that if it smelled of vomit then he could have their bed and she and Sam would be quite happy down here. He hadn't been able to smell anything then but now he can. He lies awake wondering how families manage in this awful perpetual twilight of false sleep: the landing lights left on, the rustlings and the snatches of childish sleep talk, the bare feet padding downstairs, the murmured parental admonishments, the baby's loud cry at some point, Sam's snoring, the toilet light left on after a child's visit so that the fan keeps whirring until he goes upstairs himself to switch it off. He hears one of them climb into bed with Sam and Rachel. He hears the bed creak and protest as the adults move over.

He remembers glancing into Sam and Rachel's bedroom on his way to the toilet this afternoon when he arrived. The king-size bed, its grubby Habitat striped sheets and heaped-up duvet littered with clothes and toys and Rachel's hairbrush and face cream, looked to him then like the outward embodiment of something he wanted, something he had missed out on. In the thin hours before dawn, the truth seems bleaker. He isn't a good sleeper at the best of times. The duvet is too hot and then when he pushes it off he is too cold. He finds himself longing for the perfect silence of his own room, which he thought was what he wanted to escape from, coming down here.

MOTHER'S SON

Someone told Christine that Alan was going to get married again: the new girl apparently was half his age. Christine didn't think she cared. She hardly ever spoke to Alan these days; there was no need for them to consult together over arrangements for their son, now that Thomas was grown up and made his own arrangements. In fact, after the person told her the news, at a dinner party, Christine forgot it almost at once in the noisy laughter and conversation, and only remembered it again the following afternoon, when she was sitting at home, writing.

She was making notes for a lecture on women novelists and modernism; books by Rhys and Woolf and Bowen were piled all around her, some of them open face down on the table, some of them bristling with torn bits of paper as bookmarks. When she suddenly remembered the news about Alan she lifted her mind from its entanglement in the Paris and Ireland of the twenties and stared around in surprise at her real room in London: tall and white and spacious, with thriving house plants and, filling the wall at one end, a floor-length arched window. The rooms of the flat, where Christine lived alone, were all small – bedroom, bathroom, kitchen – apart from this big one, the centre-piece. Here she worked at a long cherrywood table; when she entertained she pushed all her books and papers to one end and laid places at the other. It was March. Outside the window a bank of dark slate-grey cloud had been piled up by the wind against a lakelike area of silvery-lemon sky, smooth and translucent; the alterations in the light flowed fast, like changing expressions, across the stone housefronts opposite.

Christine's flat was on the second floor; the house was one in a row of houses all with the same phenomenal window and cold north light, built as artists' studios in the 1890s. Some had been renovated and cost the earth, like hers; others were still dilapidated, bohemian, mysterious, the windows draped with rags of patchwork and lace curtains or satin bedspreads. Inside the room, the weather and the light were always intimately present; there were long white curtains at the window but she didn't close them very often. Instead of shutting the drama out, they suggested too eloquently immense presences on the other side. It had been difficult to choose paintings for the walls; in the end Christine had hung a couple of prints of Mondrian drawings. Nothing else had seemed quite still enough.

The doorbell rang, she padded in her stocking feet to the intercom.

—Mum? It's Thomas.

She made them both coffee, hasty – measuring out the grounds, taking down the mugs – in her pleasure at his visit, her eagerness to get back to where her son, her only child, was sprawled in the low-slung white armchair in front of the window. She put milk and sugar on the tray, she was glad she had bought expensive chocolate biscuits. She found an ashtray: no one else was allowed to smoke in her flat. Thomas always for some reason chose that armchair, and then leaned his head back against the headrest so that the ridiculous length of him (he was six foot four) stretched out horizontally, almost as if he were lying flat; he crossed his ankles and squinted frowningly at his shoes.

Today he was wearing his disintegrating old trainers, not

the brogues he had for work; his unironed khaki shirt was half in and half out of his trousers. Christine, who hated uniforms, was almost ashamed at how handsome she found him in his obligatory work suit and tie; but she also loved him returned to his crumpled, worn-out old clothes, youth and beauty glowing steadily through them. Thomas was odd-looking, with a crooked nose and a big loose mouth. He hadn't bothered to get his tawny hair cut; his skin flared sensitively where the raw planes of his face were overgrowing their childish softness. From under his heavy lids, the green eyes flecked with hazel glanced lazily, like Alan's. If she thought of Alan at all these days (she hadn't seen him more than five or six times in the last twenty years), it was only when Thomas's likeness to him took her by surprise.

—So I hear your father's getting married again?

—Who told you? There was a flicker of solicitousness in his expression, in case she minded.

—Someone who knows Laura. Poor Laura.

Laura had been Alan's first wife, the one he was married to all through his affair with Christine, those long years ago. Laura had always made Thomas welcome in her home, even after Alan strayed a second time, and then a third, and then stayed away permanently. Thomas was close to his half-brothers and -sisters, and managed gracefully a whole complex of loyalties.

—I think Laura's OK, Thomas said. —I think she's pretty indifferent these days to what Dad's up to.

This wasn't what the person at the dinner party had told Christine.

—I hear the girl he's marrying is young enough to be his daughter.

Thomas couldn't help his grin: spreading, conspiratorial. He was easily entertained. —You know what he's like.

—Have you met her?

—She's OK. I reckon she knows what she's getting into.

But put it this way: I don't think it was her intellectual qualities he fell for. I thought that you might be in college today, he added. —I only came here on the off chance.

—Thursdays I usually work at home. Why aren't you in the office?

—I phoned and told them I was ill. I haven't pulled a sickie for ages. I've got a lot of stuff going round in my head and I wanted some time out to really think about it. And I thought I might stop by to have a bit of a chat about something that's cropped up.

Christine was touched: he rarely came to her to talk about his problems. In fact, there had been almost no problems. He was an affable, sociable boy whose directness was of the easy and not the exacting kind. Thomas heaved himself upright in the chair, so that his knees were jack-knifed in front of his face; he stirred two spoons of sugar into his coffee and ate chocolate biscuits.

—Is it about your dad and this wedding?

—God, no. That honestly isn't a big deal. I'm glad for him.

—Work?

He made a face. —And other stuff.

Thomas had finished at Oxford the year before and had been working as an assistant to a Labour MP, a woman, no one very special. All he did was photocopy and file and send standard answers to constituents' letters, but the idea was that this could lead to bigger and better things, some kind of political career. It was only an idea, being tested. Thomas didn't know whether a political career was what he really wanted. Christine thought he might be too finely consti-tuted, too conscientious for it. On the other hand she was proud of his realism, and that he was thinking unsentimen-tally about ways to get power and change things.

—I've got myself in a bit of a mess, Thomas said. —With Anna.

—Oh?

He fished his tobacco and rolling papers out of a pocket and used the flat tops of his knees as a table.

—I seem to have got involved with somebody else.

—Oh, Thomas.

He told her about a girl he had met at work. He said that he hadn't liked her at first – he'd thought she was too full of herself. But then they'd had to work on some assignment together and he'd got to know her a lot better. He could talk to her in a way he'd never talked to anyone else. She was very bright. She wasn't good-looking in the way Anna was good-looking.

—She's quite big, he said. —Not fat. Curvy. With this sort of messy black hair. Long.

Thomas's own hair was hanging down across his face as he rolled his cigarette, so Christine couldn't see his expression. She could hear, though, his voice thick with an excitement that she recognised as belonging to the first phase of infatuation, when even speaking about your lover, saying ordinary things about him or her, is a part of desire.

—The worst thing is, he said, shaking his hair back and looking frankly at her. —Well, not the worst thing. But they both have the same name. Not quite the same. She's called Annie.

Christine couldn't help a puff of laughter.

—I know, he said. —Shite, isn't it? He laughed with her. —The two Anns.

—Have you told Anna?

He shook his head. —I thought at first it was just, you know, nothing. Not worth upsetting her about.

—But it's something?

He shrugged and opened his hands at her in a gesture of defencelessness, squinting in the smoke from the roll-up that wagged in his mouth. How was he to know? Nothing like this had ever happened to him before.

Christine felt protective of Anna, although she had sometimes thought her too sweet and dull for Thomas. How clearly she could imagine this new girl: less pretty, overweight, clever, treacherous. These were all the things that she herself had been: she was on her guard at once, as if against a rival.

—She's different, he said. —She's funny; she makes me laugh. She doesn't take everything too seriously.

—And how do you feel about deceiving Anna?

He gulped his coffee. She saw him flooded with shame then, not able to trust himself to speak: an unpractised liar.

—These things happen, she soothed. —We can't pretend they don't. Even if we were good, if we were perfectly and completely chaste, we can't control what happens in our imagination. So being good might only be another kind of lie.

When Christine had begun her affair with Alan, there had been a possibility of his leaving his wife and family. For a while, in fact, he had left, and they had lived together. Thomas was conceived during that time. It had not worked out, they had fought horribly, and Alan had been sick with missing his children. In the end he had taken himself home. Such storms, such storms, there had been in Christine's life then: with Alan, and with others, afterwards. When she longed for her youth, those storms were what she missed, and not the happy times. The excitement of upheaval, a universe open with possibility, the phone calls that changed everything, the conspiratorial consultations with girlfriends, the feverish packing for surprise trips, escaping out of the last thing or rushing to embrace the next. Perhaps Thomas remembered some of those adventures, too: late-night train journeys when he had sat beside her with big sleepless eyes, sucking at his dummy, fingering the precious corner of his blanket, his little red suitcase packed with books and toys.

Later, once he was established at school, she had settled

into a steadier routine for his sake. But perhaps now, when he found himself infatuated and intoxicated and behaving badly, at some level of consciousness he'd recognised it as her terrain, and come to her because he thought she would know what he should do next. Perhaps his coming to her with his own crisis was a kind of forgiveness, for those upheavals.

—What about work? she said.

Thomas looked at her vaguely. Work seemed, of course, a straw, in relation to the great conflagration of his passionate life.

—You said there were work issues as well that you were worried about.

—Only the old question. I mean, here I am stuffing envelopes for an MP who voted for the war in Iraq. Should I stay inside the tent pissing out? Perhaps it would be more dignified to get out and do some pissing in.

—Dignified pissing.

—But we've been over all that so many times.

—Only now it's complicated because she's there at work? Annie.

—It would solve everything if I just took off and went away by myself to live in Prague or somewhere. Budapest.

—Leave both of them you mean? Christine said.

—Woman trouble, she sighed, making a joke of it.

She was suddenly quite sure that he would, in fact, move abroad for a while, even though he didn't know it yet himself, and it had only popped into his conversation as a joke-possibility. After much confabulation and self-interrogation and any number of painful scenes with his two girls, this was what he would do.

—I'd miss you if you moved to Prague, she said.

—Get a sabbatical. Come out and stay.

She loved having him near her in London. But as soon as she had imagined Prague she knew that it was what she wanted for him: something more than the slick game of opportunity and advancement, a broader and deeper initiation into old sophisticated Europe, into a grown-up life with complications.

—I have to go, Thomas said.

He had looked at his watch three or four times in the last fifteen minutes.

—You're meeting Annie?

—No, he lied.

Though he had made his confession to Christine, she wasn't even in imagination to follow him to wherever he was meeting his big, dark, clever girl. She was only his mother, after all. It might be Anna's night for Pilates or whatever it was she did. The lovers might have the whole evening ahead of them, after Annie had finished work, to sit in a hidden corner in a pub somewhere, crushing out cigarettes half smoked, going over and over the same broken bits of logic, pressing knees against knees under the table, getting excitedly drunker. Or to go back to her place. All that stuff.

By the time Thomas left, the sky outside Christine's window had changed again. The bank of grey-black had broken up and swallowed the lemon lake; now tousled scraps of cloud tumbled untidily in a brooding light. Christine had another hour to work before she finished for the day and showered and changed; she was meeting a friend for a film – a Bergman screening at the BFI – and a late supper. She picked up her copy of *Good Morning, Midnight*. Her name was on the flyleaf: Christine Logan, Girton College, 1971. She was certain that she had held this same copy in her hands the morning of the day that Thomas was born, in 1980 – not his birthday but the day before, since he wasn't actually born until half past midnight. She had been working on her thesis then, typing up a new chapter to show her supervisor, checking every quotation carefully against her text, when she felt the first pain.

The first pain – the first sign she'd had that Thomas was coming, two weeks before his time – had been like a sharp tiny bell struck as a signal; feeling it had been more like hearing something, a very precise high note, from deep inside her swollen abdomen, which was pressed with some difficulty into the space between her chair and the little rickety desk she worked at. None of the other things that the midwives at the hospital had warned her to expect had happened – the show of bloody mucus, or the waters breaking – only this little bell of pain, so small it was more pleasurable than unpleasant, zinging away from time to time inside her. She knew that she was supposed to delay going into the hospital for as long as she could, so she continued typing, her mind seeming to move at a pitch of high, free clarity between the words of the novel and her own extra-ordinary circumstance. All this went on in the sitting room of the little cottage she rented from Jesus College in those days, in the Kite in Cambridge. The cottage was gone now, pulled down to make way for new developments.

Once, while she waited, she had got up from the desk and stared at her face in a tarnished old junk-shop mirror she kept propped up on the mantelpiece for the sake of its frame. She thought that only fifty years before, at the time when the Rhys novel was written, she might have stared at herself like this, on the brink of the unknown ordeal, and been justified in wondering whether she would survive it. In the novel, Sasha's baby died. Christine was not afraid, exactly, but she could not imagine what lay in wait for her on the far side of the hours to come. When she was at the hospital for her antenatal appointments, she had sometimes passed new mothers walking out to a waiting car or a taxi, followed by nurses carrying their babies bundled in white shawls. She didn't have friends with babies; she didn't know what it would mean, to be responsible for a white-wrapped bundle of her own.

She had picked up the telephone once or twice to call Alan, but cut herself off before she even finished dialling. Although the plan had always been for him to be there with her at the birth of their child, for the first time the idea of his large presence bothered her: he was a big tall man with a booming voice and a curling salt-and-pepper beard, a historian, a Marxist. I can manage this by myself, she had thought that morning, timing the little bells of pain which began to ring louder and stronger. It was as if she had intuited with the first pang of Thomas's arrival, and quite rightly, that her delighted possession of her son would push apart whatever mechanism it was that had bound her to his father for those years of her youth.

Christine's thesis was on certain women writers of the early twentieth century. She had argued that in their novels and stories they had broken with the conventions deep-buried in the foundations of the fiction tradition: that all good stories end in marriage, and that the essential drive in plot is courtship, bringing men and women together. Katherine Mansfield's *femmes seules* and Woolf's solitaries represented a break that was at least as revolutionary, surely, as Lawrence's and Joyce's iconoclasm. In the late seventies, the automatic gesture of obeisance to feminism had not yet been internalised among academics, and an amused hostility was still the norm. Alan wouldn't read Christine's work then: he said once that he took no interest in the nuances of bourgeois ladies' hypersensibility. She had tolerated this atti-tude, at least at first; she had even been attracted by it, as if in his contemptuous maleness he were a huge handsome bear whose ferocity she had to take on, and tame, and teach.

When Thomas was four or five years old he had asked her once if he was going to die. She wasn't sure where this exchange had taken place – on a beach perhaps, although not on a summer day. She associated it vaguely with a windy walk across pale pebbles that were awkward underfoot, along the sea's rim of crisp-dried detritus: seaweed, plastic netting, bird bones. Perhaps it was on one of their trips to the Norfolk coast with Alan when he and she were still seeing each other.

She must have been carrying Thomas. She remembered his weight slipping on her hip.

—It's all right, Christine said. —Don't worry about dying. Maybe by the time you grow up they'll have invented some medicine so you won't have to.

She remembered Alan stopping abruptly. Perhaps she put Thomas down then and he went to dabble in the sea-rubbish.

—I can't believe you just said that.

He was laughing, but she thought with certainty at that moment: He hates me. The conviction reverberated like a blow against armour; she tasted blood and she wanted to fight.

—What's wrong with saying it? I used to think that when I was a little girl.

—But it isn't true.

—Of course it's not true. It's something reassuring to keep you going until you're old enough. You know, like Heaven.

—If any adult had ever lied to me about anything so important, when I found out the truth I'd never have forgiven them.

She was shocked at herself, for a moment: she wondered if he was right. Then, recovering, she mocked him.

—But that's just what you're like, isn't it? You love to go around not forgiving people for things. How austere and rigorous it must make you feel. What a little prig of a child you must have been.

He opened his mouth to answer, closed it, and turned to stride away from her down the beach. She hurried raggedly after him, not finished, snatching Thomas up from whatever he was interested in: threading washed-up ring pulls on his fingers or poking a dead gull with a stick. In her memory a wind came whipping up, tearing out her words.

—So what would you have told him, then? If you're so truthful.

He wanted to keep his mouth shut against her but he couldn't resist giving his opinion, beautifully expressed. There had been a time when she would have hung on these words of his devotedly. —I'd tell him that without death life would be formless. That change is the life force.

Christine burst out with a loud snort of laughter. —Well, try that then! Just try it. What d'you think about that, Thomas? Daddy says you have to die, but not to worry. It will give your life a nicer shape.

Thomas gave a rather stagy mew of despair, as if in fact he'd lost interest in the subject, and snuggled his head reproachfully against Christine's lapel. Alan thought Christine encouraged him to be precocious. He walked away from them now, faster than they could follow, his shoulders in his black greatcoat bowed against the wind, head down, his hair blowing out behind. Then for a while he turned round and walked backwards, facing them, looking at them. Christine couldn't remember if that argument had actually been the end of things, or if they'd made a truce later that afternoon or that night, in whatever hotel or rented cottage they were staying in, and gone on patching things up for a while longer.

The morning after Thomas's visit, Christine was climbing the stairs to her office at the university when someone came running up below her.

—Dr Logan?

Christine paused, resting her pile of books and papers on the banister; someone young with a blonde head lifted to look up at her came around the stairwell with a clatter of heels.

—Dr Logan? Do you mind if I just talk to you for a moment?

Because she was expecting a student with a query about an essay, there was a disconcerting lapse of seconds before Christine registered that the blonde head belonged to Anna, Thomas's girlfriend, whom she'd known for three years. Of course, there was no reason for Anna, who worked in the wardrobe department at English National Opera, to be on campus: she had never been there before. Also, she had never called Christine Dr Logan.

—Anna, darling, how lovely to see you. Whatever are you doing here? How did you find me?

—I want to talk about Tom.

In one smooth movement, feeling in her bag for her office keys, Christine decided that her first loyalty was to Thomas's confidence. She turned on Anna a look wiped clear of any foreknowledge.

—Is something wrong?

Anna's face was guilelessly open, sorrow stamped on it like a black bootprint. She could not speak until Christine had her door open and they were safely inside. Under the posters and potted plants Christine put the kettle on – Anna nodded an indifferent assent – to make peppermint tea. Anna pressed her palms against her cheeks: her hands were big and pink and sensitive, like her ears, with fingertips reddened from sewing.

—He's seeing someone else.

At least Christine wouldn't pretend not to take her seriously.

—Tell me about it.

—I mean, I don't have any proof. Just the usual silly stuff.

Times he's late coming home, things he says he's doing that don't sound quite right. Just something: like he's all the time slightly impatient with me, but then he's sorry for that and covering it up by being extra nice. I just know the way Tom would be if he were doing it.

—It could be nothing. I know he's the nicest boy in the world, but underneath all that he can be moody.

—I actually thought he might have talked to you. I know he came to see you yesterday. I haven't spoken to anyone else about this.

Anna had always treated Christine with tender respect. Now she scanned her intently with strained-open blue eyes, careless in her desperation. Love, this destroying kind of love, swelled the girl up, gave her a ferocity and an authority that Christine had never seen in her before.

She shook her head sympathetically. —He talked about work.

—He didn't say anything about me that struck you?

—He worries about whether he's doing the right thing, in his job.

—Is that all? Are you sure? I have to know what he's thinking.

—He's bored stuffing envelopes for someone he doesn't believe in.

Anna sighed, frowning impatiently at Christine, or through her: she would know what she was looking for when she found it, and it wasn't this. She wasn't convinced that Christine was telling the whole truth. A pressured moment swayed in the air between them: Anna jostling roughly for more, Christine blandly resisting.

—He did mention wanting to travel in Europe. But I don't know how serious that was.

—You see. I've not heard anything about that. Where in Europe exactly? When? Who with?

—He was probably only talking about a holiday.

Budapest, perhaps? He didn't say anything about who with.

—There. You see?

—I suppose I simply took it that he meant alone.

Anna stood up from the swivel office chair and turned to stare out of the window at nothing, below: a nowhere space between the Humanities block and Social Sciences, furnished with a few benches and young trees. She was tall, the same height as Christine, but with a figure that Christine had never had: high full round breasts, a narrow graspable waist, long slender haunches that suggested some graceful running creature, a gazelle. Between her short cut-off top and the absurdly low waistband of her trousers was a long expanse of flawless goosefleshed golden skin, curving into a sweet round rump. The clothes seemed incidental; Anna's young nakedness was in the room between them. With a sharpness almost like longing, Christine was aware of Anna's piercings, even now that her back was turned: in her nose and her belly button, gold rings with little ruby-coloured beads. These young women didn't know what they had. They suffered because they couldn't have Thomas to keep, but they had the struggle over him, the game of pursuit and being pursued, and the sometime possession of him in the flesh. For as long as the thought lasted, that snatched possession felt to Christine like the only thing worth living for: a possibility of joy that was no longer available to the mothers of these children.

Anna turned from the window. Her face was blotched an ugly red with tears.

—What would you do?

—Well, I'd ask him, Christine said at once. —Don't you think that he'll tell you the truth?

—Yes, Anna said bleakly. —I expect he will.

At home Christine prepared an omelette for her supper. She washed lettuce hearts and vine tomatoes; she sliced cucumber and made a vinaigrette. She mashed parsley into a lump of butter with lemon juice, and sautéed a little tinned tuna in a pan with finely chopped shallots. When all this was ready she broke the eggs into a bowl, to beat them. The second egg had gone bad. It felt strange to the touch, the shell weak and scabbed, but even as she registered this it was too late – she had cracked the egg against the side of the bowl and a foul greenish liquid poured out between her fingers, the thin texture of water, not albumen. A stink of putrefaction thrust wildly, rudely, into the kitchen.

She didn't know what to do; she pressed her mouth and nose against her sleeve, not pulling the shell apart any further, not wanting to see inside. The mess was too awful, too violently offensive, to pour down the drain; it would surely come back at her, and perhaps at her neighbours, for hours afterwards. She found an empty peanut-butter jar with a lid, saved for recycling, tipped the whole lot into that, and screwed the lid on, only half allowing herself to look at it. Then she ran downstairs out of her flat to the bins outside, where she buried the jar deep among the rubbish bags.

Upstairs she opened all the windows, even though it was raining, ran water for long minutes down the sink. She bleached the egg bowl and the dishcloth she had used to wipe up the few drops of egg that had spattered on the counter; she washed her hands in the bathroom over and over. Still, every time she put her fingers to her nose she was haunted by the smell. The thought of the rest of her supper nauseated her; she tipped the salad and the tuna into the bin. She knew she was being irrational; she ought to phone a friend and make a joke out of her small disaster, and perhaps go out for a drink and something to eat. Instead she abandoned herself to sulking, lying on her side on the sofa, her hands clasped between her knees. The idea came to her out of nowhere that there would be a last time that she brought anyone home to make love in her bed. It was not yet, it might not be for years, but it would come, even though she might not recognise it until long afterwards.

How could Christine envy Thomas's two girls? Who could want to be one of the two foolish Anns, desperate for him? Or to be Alan, with his beard shaven and his silvery hair clipped close to his skull, hoping to start out on the adventure of passion all over again? How much happier she was, how much less time and energy it took to be Thomas's mother: a relationship founded on one fixed and unalterable truth. Outside her spectacular arched window the wind threw rain in long ragged gusts across the housefronts and tore at the estate agents' signs, setting them flapping in crazy ecstasy. Christine told herself that she was glad she was on this side of the glass, but she lay still on her sofa for a long time, and after a while she turned her back on the view.

BUCKETS OF BLOOD

The coach journey from Cambridge to Bristol took six hours. Hilary Culvert was wearing a new purple skirt, a drawstring crêpe blouse and navy school cardigan, and over them her school mac, because it was the only coat she had. The year was 1972. In the toilets at Oxford bus station where they were allowed to get out she had sprayed on some perfume and unplaited her hair. She worried that she smelled of home. She didn't know quite what home smelled like, as she still lived there and was used to it; but when her sister Sheila had come back from university for Christmas she had complained about it.

—You'd think with all these children, Sheila had said, —that at least the place would smell of something freshly nasty. Feet or sweat or babies or something. But it smells like old people. Mothballs and Germolene: who still uses mothballs apart from here?

Hilary had been putting Germolene on her spots; this was the family orthodoxy. She put the little tube aside in horror. Sheila had looked so different, even after only one term away. She had always been braver about putting on a public show than Hilary was: now she wore gypsy clothes, scrumpled silky skirts and patchwork tops with flashing pieces of mirror sewn in. Her red-brown hair was fluffed out in a mass. She had insisted on washing her hair almost every day, even though this wasn't easy in the vicarage: the old Ascot gas heater only dribbled out hot water, and there

39

were all the younger children taking turns each night for baths. Their father had remonstrated with Sheila.

—There's no one here to admire you in your glory, he said. —You'll only frighten the local boys. Save your efforts until you return to the fleshpots.

—I'm not doing it for anyone to admire, said Sheila. —I'm doing it for myself.

He was a tall narrow man, features oversized for the fine bones of his face, eyes elusive behind thick-lensed glasses; he smiled as if he was squinting into a brash light. His children hadn't been brought up to flaunt doing things for themselves, although the truth was that in a family of nine a certain surreptitious selfishness was essential for survival.

Now Hilary in her half-term week was going to visit Sheila in the fleshpots, or at Bristol University, where she was reading Classics. A lady with permed blue-white hair in the seat next to her was knitting baby clothes in lemon-yellow nylon wool which squeaked on her needles; Hilary had to keep her head turned to stare out of the window because she suffered terribly from travel sickness. She wouldn't ever dream of reading on a coach, and even the flickering of the knitting needles could bring it on. The lady had tried to open up a conversation about her grand-children and probably thought Hilary was rude and unfriendly. And that was true too, that was what the Culverts were like: crucified by their shyness and at the same time contemptuous of the world of ordinary people they couldn't talk to. Outside the window there was nothing to justify her fixed attention. The sky seemed never to have lifted higher all day than a few feet above the ground; rolls of mist hung above the sodden grass like dirty wool. The signs of spring coming seemed suspended in a spasm of unfor-giving frozen cold. It should have been a relief to leave the flatlands of East Anglia behind and cross into the hills and valleys of the west, but everywhere today seemed equally colourless. Hilary didn't care. Her anticipation burned up brightly enough by itself. Little flames of it licked up inside her. This was the first time she had been away from home alone. Sheila was ahead of her in their joint project: to get as far away from home as possible, and not to become anything like their mother.

At about the same time that Sheila and Hilary had confided to each other that they didn't any longer believe in God, they had also given up believing that the pattern of domestic life they had been brought up inside was the only one, or was even remotely desirable. Somewhere else people lived differently; didn't have to poke their feet into clammy hand-me-down wellingtons and sandals marked by size inside with felt-tip pen; didn't have to do their home-work in bed with hot-water bottles because the storage heaters in the draughty vicarage gave out such paltry warmth. Other people didn't have to have locked money boxes for keeping safe anything precious, or have to sleep with the keys on string around their necks; sometimes anyway they came home from school to find those locks picked or smashed. (The children didn't tell on one another; that was their morality. But they hurt one another pretty badly, physically, in pursuit of justice. It was an honour code rather than anything resembling Christian empathy or charity.) Other people's mothers didn't stoop their heads down in the broken way that theirs did, hadn't given up on completed sentences or consecutive dialogue, didn't address elliptical ironical asides to their soup spoons as they ate.

Their mother sometimes looked less like a vicar's wife than a wild woman. She was as tall as their father but if the two of them were ever accidentally seen standing side by side it looked as if she had been in some terrible momen-tous fight for her life and he hadn't. Her grey-black hair stood out in a stiff ruff around her head; Sheila said she must cut it with the kitchen scissors in the dark. She had some kind of palsy so that her left eye drooped; there were bruise-coloured wrinkled shadows under her eyes and beside her hooked nose. Her huge deflated stomach and bosom were slapped like insults on to a girl's bony frame. She was fearless in the mornings about stalking round the house in her ancient baggy underwear, big pants and maternity bra, chasing the little ones to get them dressed: her older children fled the sight of her. They must have all counted, without confessing it to one another: she was forty-nine, Patricia was four. At least there couldn't be any more pregnancies, so humiliating to their suffering adolescence.

As girls, Sheila and Hilary had to be especially careful to make their escape from home. Their older brother Andrew had got away, to do social policy at York and join the Young Socialists, which he told them was a Trotskyite entrist group. He was never coming back, they were sure of it. He hadn't come back this Christmas. But their sister Sylvia had married an RE teacher at the local secondary modern school who was active in their father's church and in the local youth clubs. Sylvia already had two babies, and Sheila and Hilary had heard her muttering things to herself. They remembered that she used to be a jolly sprightly girl even if they hadn't liked her much: competitive at beach rounders when they went on day trips to the coast, sentimentally devoted to the doomed stray dogs she tried to smuggle into their bedroom. Now, when they visited her rented flat in Haverhill, her twin-tub washing machine was always pulled out from the wall, filling the kitchen with urine-pungent steam. Sylvia would be standing uncommunicatively, heaving masses of boiling nappies with wooden tongs out of the washer into the spin tub, while the babies bawled in the battered wooden playpen that had been handed on from the vicarage.

In the coach, aware of her reflection in the window from

time to time when the scenery was dun enough behind to make a mirror out of it, Hilary sat up very straight. She and Sheila had practised with one another, remembering never to lapse into the crumpled unawareness that smote their mother if ever for a moment she left off being busy. She was almost always busy. She had driven Hilary in to catch her coach that morning only because she had to go in to Cambridge anyway, to buy replacement school shorts and other uniform from Eaden Lilley for the boys. The boys had larked around in the back seats of the ropy old Bedford van that was their family transport, kicking at each other's shins and dropping to wriggle on their bellies about the floor, so that their mother – who drove badly anyway, with grindings of the gears and sudden brakings – spent the whole journey deploring fruitlessly, and peering to try and locate them in the rear-view mirror. She had taken to wearing dark glasses when she went anywhere outside her home, to cover up the signs of her palsy. She stopped the van on Parker's Piece and had to get out to open the door on Hilary's side because the handle was broken. Hilary had a vivid idea of how her mother must appear to strangers: the sticking-up hair and dark glasses and the worn once-good coat she never had time to button up; her jerky burrowing movements, searching for money or lists in bags or under the van seats; her cut-glass enunciations, without eye contact, of bits of sentences that never became any whole message. When Hilary walked away with her suitcase to take her place in the little huddled crowd of waiting travellers she wouldn't look to see if any of them had been watching.

Bristol bus station was a roaring cavern: everything was greasy and filthy with oil, including the maimed pigeons. Green double-decker city buses reversed out of the bays and rumbled off, important with illumination, into the evening.

A whole day's light had come and gone on the journey. Hilary looked excitedly for Sheila while she shuffled down the aisle on the coach. She wasn't worried that she couldn't see her right away. 'Whatever you do don't go off anywhere,' Sheila had instructed her. 'Stay there till I come.'

Someone waited slouching against the metal railing while she queued for her suitcase, then stepped forward to confront her when she had it: a young man, short and soft-bodied, with lank light brown hair and a half-grown beard, wearing a pinstriped suit jacket over jeans. He also had bare feet, and black eye make-up.

—Are you Hilary?

He spoke with a strong northern accent.

Hilary felt the disapproving attention of the blue-rinsed knitting lady, focused on his make-up and his feet. She disdained the disapproval, even though in the same instant she judged against the man with Culvert passionate finality. 'What an unappealing little dwarf of a chap,' she thought, in her mother's voice. Of course her thought didn't show. To him she would look only like the sum of what she was outwardly: pale with bad skin, fatally provincial, frightened, with girls' school gushing manners.

—Yes.

—Sheila couldn't be here. She's unwell. You have to come with me.

He swung away without smiling or otherwise acknowledging her; he had only ever looked perfunctorily in her face, as if he was checking basics. She had to follow after him, out through the bus station back entrance into a twilit cobbled street and then up right beside a high grim wall that curved round to join a busier road. The tall buildings of a hospital with their lighted windows rose sobering and impassive against the evening sky, where the murky day in its expiring was suddenly brilliantly deep clear blue, studded already with one or two points of stars. The man walked ahead and Hilary followed, hurrying, struggling with her suitcase, three or four steps behind. The suitcase was an old leather one embossed with her grandfather's intials; he had taken it to ecumenical conferences in the thirties. Because the clasps were liable to spring open she had fastened an elastic Brownie belt around it.

Unwell! Unwell was the word they had to use to the games mistress at school when they weren't having showers because they had a period. Hilary saved the joke up to amuse Sheila. Then she was flooded with doubt; why had she followed this rude man so obediently? She should have at least questioned him, asked him where Sheila was and what was wrong with her. Sheila had told her to wait, whatever happened, at the bus station. She opened her mouth to protest to him, to demand that he explain to her, and take a turn carrying the case. Then stubbornly she closed it again. She knew what a squeak would come out of it if she tried to attract his attention while she was struggling along like this. And if she put the case down and stopped she was afraid he'd go on without noticing she was no longer behind him, and then she would be truly lost in an unknown city, with nowhere to spend the night, and certainly not enough money to pay for anywhere. She could perhaps have hired a taxi to take her to Sheila's hall of residence, although she wasn't sure what that would cost either. She had never been in a taxi in her life, and would never have the courage to try and signal to one. And what if Sheila wasn't at the hall of residence?

Pridefully she marched on, though her breath was hurting in her chest and her hand without its glove – they were somewhere in her shoulder bag but she couldn't stop to find them – was freezing into a claw on the case handle. Her arm felt as if it was being dragged from her shoulder. It wasn't clothes that made her case heavy, but some books Sheila had asked her to bring. Every forty paces – she began to count – she swapped her case and shoulder bag from hand to hand, and that gave a few moments of relief. She fixed her eyes on the back of the rumpled pinstriped jacket. Once or twice, on the zebra crossings, he looked back to check for her. Luckily his bare feet seemed to slow him down somewhat, probably because he had to keep an eye out for what he might be walking in. There were quite a few people on the streets, even though the shops were closed; sometimes he held back to let a crowd go by, perhaps because he was afraid of someone stepping on his toes. Perversely Hilary started slowing down too whenever this happened. She was damned now if she wanted to catch up with him. Even if he stopped to wait for her, now, she thought that she would stop too and wait, as if the distance between them had become a fixed relationship, an invisible rigid frame of air connecting them and holding them apart in the same grip.

She thought she recognised the streets that they were walking through. When their father had driven Sheila over with her things at the start of the autumn term, Hilary had come with them; she had wanted to be able to picture where Sheila was, when she wasn't at home. This shopping area was on a hill behind the city centre: it had seemed lively and fashionable, with tiny boutiques, cafés, a department store whose long glass windows were stuck with brown and yellow paper leaves. She had seen Sheila taking it all in from her front seat in the van, satisfied with her choice, impatient to be left alone to explore. At home they could only ever get lifts in to Cambridge every so often, and anyway their shopping there was dogged by waiting parents, ready with ironic comments on whatever the girls chose to buy with their money. Dimly in the dusk now, Hilary could see the Victorian Gothic university tower where it ought to be, over to her right. Manor Hall residence where Sheila had a room should be somewhere off to the left, up past a little triangle of green grass. The pinstriped jacket struck off left, and Hilary was relieved. They must arrive soon, and she would be able to put her case down, and be rid of her dreadful companion.

The road he took didn't lead up past any triangle of grass but downhill; it was wide, busy with fast through traffic but not with people. They left the shops behind and it seemed all at once to be completely night; the pavement ran alongside a daunting high wall to their left. The steep hills and old high walls of this city were suddenly sinister and not quaint, as if they hid dark prisons and corruptions in their folds. Hilary followed the pinstriped jacket in a grim, fixed despair. In spite of the cold she was sweating, and her chest was racked. She thought that catastrophe had overtaken her. She had made an appalling mistake when she meekly followed this man out of the bus station, like a trusting child, like an idiot. The only form of dignity left to her was not to falter, or make a worse fool of herself screaming and running, not to break the form of the rigid relationship in which they moved. She thought he might be taking her somewhere to kill her with a knife. She wouldn't say a word to save her life; she might swing at him with her grandfather's suitcase. Or she imagined drugs, which she didn't know anything about: perhaps drug addicts recruited new associates by bundling strangers into their den and injecting them with heroin. She didn't ever imagine rape or anything of that sort, because she thought that as a preliminary to that outrage there would have to be some trace of interest in her, some minimal sign of a response to her, however disgusted.

The pinstriped jacket crossed the road, darting between cars. Following, Hilary hardly cared if she was hit. He struck off up a narrow precipitous hill with tall toppling houses facing on to the pavement on either side. Because of the effort of climbing she had her head down and almost walked into him when he stopped outside a front door. He pushed the door and it swung open. The house inside was dark.

—In here, he said, and led the way.

Hilary followed.

In the hall he switched on a light: a bare bulb hung from the ceiling. The place was desolate: ancient wallpaper washed to colourlessness hung down in sheets from the walls. Even in her extremity, though, she could tell that this had been an elegant house once. City lights twinkled through a tall arched window. The stairs wound round and round a deep stairwell, up into blackness; the handrail was smooth polished wood. Everything smelled of a mineral decay. They climbed up two flights, their footsteps echoing because there was no stair carpet. He pushed another door.

—She's in there.

Hilary didn't know what she expected to find.

Sheila was sitting with a concentrated face, rocking backwards and forwards on a double bed which was just a mattress on bare floorboards. She was wearing a long black T-shirt, her hair was scraped carelessly back and tied with a scarf. The room was lit by another bare bulb, not a ceiling pendant this time but a lamp-base without a shade, which cast leering shadows upwards. It was warm: an electric radiator painted mustard yellow was plugged in the same socket as the lamp. Hilary felt herself overheating at once, her face turning hot red, after her exertions in the cold outside.

—Thank God you've come, Hills, Sheila said.

She sounded practical rather than emotional. That at least was reassuring.

Pinstripe stepped into the room behind Hilary. He put on a shifty uncomfortable smile, not quite looking straight at Sheila, focusing on the dark tangle of sheets and blankets that she seemed to have kicked to the bottom of the bed.

—D'you want anything? Tea?

Sheila shook her head. —I'm only throwing it up.

—D'you want anything?

Hilary couldn't believe he was actually talking to her. —No, I'm fine, thanks, she said.

—I'll be downstairs, he said. —If you need anything.

They heard the sound of his footsteps retreating. Hilary put down her case: her hand for quite a few minutes wouldn't ease from its frozen curled position. —Shuggs: what's going on?

Sheila groaned: not in answer to the question, but a sound ripped from inside her, a low and embarrassing rumble as if she didn't care what anybody heard. She rocked fiercely.

—I'm miscarrying a pregnancy, she said when the spasm seemed to have passed. —It's a fine mess. Blood everywhere. Buckets of blood. You'll have to help get rid of everything.

—I can't believe this, Hilary said. She felt she was still somewhere inside the Bluebeard story she had been imagining on her way from the bus station. For a few pure moments she blazed with anger against Sheila. It wasn't fair, for Sheila to have spoiled her visit with this, her so looked-forward-to chance to get away. Sheila's mission had been clear and certain: to cut herself free of all the muffling dependencies of home and childhood. If she could succumb to anything so predictable as this melodrama – just what their parents would have warned against if only they hadn't been too agonised to find the words – what hope was there?

—What are you doing here? she demanded. —What is this place?

—It's a squat, said Sheila calmly. —Neil's squat. I told them at Manor Hall that I was going away for a few days. They're not to ever know anything about this, obviously.

—You'd be kicked out.

—Uh-oh, said Sheila, attentive to something inside her. Then she lunged from the bed to sit on something like a chamber pot in the crazy shadows on the far side of the room. Hilary tried not to hear anything. —Oh, oh, Sheila groaned, hugging her white legs, pressing her forehead to her knees.

—They wouldn't kick me out, she said after a while. —It's not that.

—And who's Neil?

—That's him, you idiot. You've just walked in with him.

Hilary hadn't moved from where she stood when she first came in, or even made any move to unbutton her mac. She felt as if there was an unpassable waste of experience between her and her sister now, which couldn't be crossed. Sheila had joined the ranks of women submerged and knowing amid their biology. She realised with a new shock that Sheila must have had sexual intercourse, too, in order to be pregnant.

—I don't want Mum to know, that's why, Sheila said. —I'll simply kill you if you ever tell anyone at home.

—I wouldn't, said Hilary coldly.

—I just can't bear the idea of her thinking that this is the same thing, you know? The same stuff that's happened to her. Because it isn't.

Hilary was silent. After a long while Sheila stood up stiffly from the chamber pot. She stuffed what looked like an old towel between her legs, and moving slowly, bent over as if she was very old, she lay down on the bed again, on her side this time, with her eyes closed.

—You could take it down to the lavatory for me. It's a flight and a half down, door on the right.

Hilary didn't stir.

—Please, Hills. You could cover it with a newspaper or something.

—Did you do this deliberately? Hilary said. —Is this an abortion?

—No. It just happened. I might have done it deliberately, but I didn't need to. I'd only just realised that I was pregnant. I've only missed two periods, I think. I never keep track.

—Who is the father of it?

Sheila's eyes snapped open incredulously. —Who do you think? she said. —I wouldn't have just sent any old person to get you.

Hilary helped. Several times she carried the chamber pot down one and a half flights of stairs, holding the banister rail, watching her feet carefully in the gloom (there was only the one bulb in the hallway, which Neil had switched on when they first came in). She covered whatever was inside the pot with a piece of newspaper, then tipped it into the lavatory without looking and flushed the chain. Thankfully it had a good strong flush. She stood listening to voices downstairs, a long way off as if they came from underground, from a basement room perhaps: Neil's voice and others, male and female, subdued but nonetheless breaking out into laughter sometimes. Opening off the landing above the lavatory Hilary found a filthy bathroom, with a torn plastic curtain at the window, overgrown with black mould. An ancient rusted red-painted reel wound with canvas rope was secured to the wall beside the window, with instructions on how to lower it as an escape harness in case of fire. She ran the bath taps for a while, but although the pipes gave out buckings and bellowing noises and hiccuped gouts of tea-coloured cold water into the grit and dirt in the bottom of the bath, she couldn't get either tap to run hot.

—There's no hot water, Sheila said. —This is a squat: what did you think? Everyone goes into the halls to bathe. We're lucky to have electricity: one of the guys knew how to reconnect it. You could ask Neil for the electric kettle. What do you want hot water for anyway?

—I thought you might like a wash. I thought I could put some things in to soak.

—Don't worry about it. I'll wash in the morning. We can take all this stuff to the launderette later.

Although they had always lived so close together in the forced intimacy of the vicarage, where there was only one lavatory and fractious queues for the bathroom in the mornings, the sisters had been prudish in keeping their bodily functions hidden from one another. This was partly in scalded reaction to their mother, who poked curiously in the babies' potties to find swallowed things, and delivered sanitary towels to the girls' room with abandoned openness, as if she didn't know that the boys saw. They had even always, since they stopped being little girls, undressed quickly with their backs turned, or underneath their nightdresses. It was a surprise how small the step seemed, once Hilary had taken it, over into this new bodily intimacy of shared secret trouble and mess. Sheila's pains, she began to understand, had a rhythm to them: first a strong pang, then a pause, then a sensation as if things were coming away inside her. After that she might get ten or fifteen minutes' respite. When the pain was at its worst, Hilary rubbed her back, or Sheila gripped her hand and squeezed it, hard and painfully, crushing the bones together.

—Damn, damn, damn, she swore in a sing-song moan while she rocked backwards and forwards; tears squeezed out of her shut eyes and ran down her cheeks.

—Are you sorry? Hilary said, humbled.

—How could I possibly be sorry? Sheila snapped. —You think I want a *baby*?

She said the pains had begun at three in the afternoon. She told Hilary at some point that if they were still going on in the morning they would have to call an ambulance and get her into hospital: she explained in a practical voice that women could haemorrhage and die if these things went wrong. By ten o'clock, though, the worst seemed to be over. There hadn't been any bad pains for over an hour, the bleeding was almost like a normal period. When Neil came upstairs Sheila wanted a cup of tea and a hot-water bottle.

—You'll have to take Hilary out, she told him, —and buy her something to eat.

Hilary had eaten some sandwiches on the coach at lunchtime. She hadn't had anything since then; she didn't feel hungry but she felt light-headed and her hands were shaking.

—I'm fine, she said hastily. —I don't want anything.

—Don't be so silly. Buy her some fish and chips or something.

Hilary was too tired not to be obedient. She put on her mac and followed Neil downstairs, as if their fatal passage round the city had to recommence. At least this time she wouldn't be carrying her case. She waited on the street outside; he said he had to fetch the others.

—By the way, he added, not looking at her, —I shouldn't mention anything. They just think Sheila's got a tummy bug. They'd be upset.

—OK, Hilary mumbled. Furiously she thought to herself that she wouldn't have spoken to his friends about her sister if he had tortured her. 'You silly little man,' she imagined herself saying. 'How dare you think I care about upsetting them?' She tipped back her head and looked up the precipitous fronts of the houses to the far-off sky, studded with cold stars.

She noticed that Neil had put on shoes to come out this time: a pair of gym shoes, gaping without laces. His friend Julian had jug ears and long dyed blond hair; Gus was shy and lumpish, like a boy swelled to man-size without his face or body actually changing to look grown-up. Becky was a pretty girl in a duffel coat, who giggled and swivelled her gaze too eagerly from face to face: she couldn't get enough of her treat, being the only girl and having the attention of three men. She knew instinctively that Hilary didn't count. Even her patronising was perfunctory: she reminisced about her own A levels as if she was reaching back into a long-ago past.

—You've chosen all the easy ones, you clever thing! My school forced me to do double maths, it was ghastly.

—Are you sure you're not hungry? Neil said to Hilary as they hurried past a busy chip shop with a queue. —Only if we don't stop we're in time for the pub. You could have some crisps there.

Hilary gazed into the bright steamy window, assaulted by the smell of the chips, weak with longing. —Quite sure, she said. She had never been into a pub in her life. There was a place in Haverhill where some of the girls went from school, but she and Sheila had always despised the silly self-importance of teenage transgression. It was impossible to imagine ever wanting to enter the ugly square red-brick pub in the village, where the farm labourers drank, and the men from the estate who worked in the meat-packing factory. Neil's pub was a tiny cosy den, fumy light glinting off the rows of glasses and bottles. The stale breath of it made Hilary's head swim; they squeezed into red plush seats around a table. Neil didn't ask her what she wanted, but brought her a small mug of brown beer and a packet of crisps and one of peanuts. She didn't like the taste of the beer but because the food was so salty she drank it in thirsty mouthfuls, and then was seized by a sensation as if she floated up to hang some little way above her present situation, graciously indifferent, so that her first experience of drunkenness was a blessed one.

When the pub closed they came back to the house and sat around a table in the basement kitchen by candlelight: the kitchen walls were painted crudely with huge mushrooms and blades of grass and giant insects, making Hilary feel as if she was a miniature human at the deep bottom of a forest. She drank the weak tea they put in front of her. The others talked about work and exams. Becky was doing biological sciences, Gus was doing history, Julian and Neil seemed to be doing English. Hilary couldn't believe that they sounded just like girls at school, scurrying in the rat-run of learning and testing, trying to outdo one another in protestations of how little work they'd done. Not once did any of them actually speak seriously about their subjects. Hilary felt so deeply disappointed in university life that on the spot she made up her mind to dedicate herself to something different and nobler, although she wasn't clear what. Neil and Julian were concentrating upon sticking a brown lump of something on a pin and roasting it with a match. From her indifferent distance she supposed this must be drugs, but she wasn't frightened of that now.

—Don't tell your daddy the vicar what you've seen, said Neil.

She was confused – did the others know what had happened after all? – until she realised that he meant the brown lump.

—Are you two really from a vicarage? asked Becky. —It's like something out of a book.

—We can't offer the respectability that Hilary's used to, Neil said. —She'll have to slum it here for a few days.

Hilary could see that Neil was the centre of all the others' attention. At least he had not joined in when the others were fluttering and fussing about their work; he had smiled to himself, licking the edges of little pieces of white paper and sticking them together as if none of it bothered him. He had an air as if he saw through the sham of it all, as if he came from a place where the university didn't count for much: she could see how this had power over the others. He didn't say much but when he spoke it was with a deliberate debunking roughness that made the others abject, ashamed even of the feel in their mouths of their own nice eager voices.

Becky told Neil flirtatiously that he would have to be on his best behaviour, while Hilary was staying. —No swearing, she said. —'Cause I can see she's a nice girl.

—Fuck, he said. —I hadn't thought of that. Fuck that.

Hilary thought of the farm boys at home, who called sexual words when she and Sheila had to walk past them in their school uniform. She had always thought, however much it tortured her, that they had an obscure right to do it because of their work. In the winter mornings from the school bus you could see the frozen mists rising up out of the flat colourless fields, and figures bent double with sacks across their shoulders, picking Brussels sprouts, or sugar beeting. But Neil was here, wasn't he, at university? He'd crossed over to their side, the lucky side. Whatever she thought of her life, she knew it was on the lucky side, so long as she wasn't picking Brussels sprouts or meat-packing.

No one had said anything since she arrived about where Hilary was to sleep. Sheila was supposed to have booked a guest room for her at Manor Hall, but of course she couldn't go there now. When she couldn't hold herself upright at the kitchen table any longer she climbed upstairs to ask what she should do, but Sheila was asleep, breathing evenly and deeply. Her forehead was cool. Hilary kept all her clothes on and wrapped herself in an old quilt that Sheila had kicked off; she curled up to sleep on the floor beside the bed. At some point in the night she woke, frozen rigid and harrowed by a bitter draught blowing up through the bare floorboards; she climbed into the bed beside Sheila who snorted and heaved over. Under the duvet and all the blankets it smelled of sweat and blood, but it was warm. When she woke again it was morning and the sun was shining.

—Look at the patterns, Sheila said.

She was propped up calmly on one elbow on the pillow, and seemed returned into her usual careful self-possession. Hilary noticed for the first time that the room was painted yellow; the sun struck through the tall uncurtained windows and projected swimming squares of light on to the walls, dancing with the movements of the twiggy tops of trees which must be growing in a garden outside.

—Are you all right? she asked.

Sheila ignored the question as if there had never been anything wrong.

—How did you get on with everybody last night?

—We went to a pub.

—Oh, which one? She interrogated Hilary until she was satisfied that it must have been the Beaufort. —We often go there, she said enthusiastically. —It's got a great atmosphere, it's really local.

—When I told them we lived in a vicarage, Hilary said, —one of them asked if we were Catholics.

—That's so funny. I bet I know who that was. What did you think of Neil?

Hilary was cautious. —Is he from the north?

—Birmingham, you idiot. Couldn't you tell? Such a pure Brummie accent.

—He wasn't awfully friendly.

Sheila smiled secretively. —He doesn't do that sort of small talk. His dad works as a toolsetter at Lucas's, the engineering company. No one in his family has been to university before. His parents don't have money, compared to most of the students here. He gets pretty impatient with people, you know, who just take their privilege for granted.

Hilary felt like a child beside her sister. What had happened yesterday marked Sheila as initiated into the adult world, apart from her, as clearly as if she was signed with blood on her forehead. She supposed it must be the unknown of sexual intercourse which could transform things in this way that children couldn't see: Neil's self-importance into power, for instance. At the same time as she was in awe of her sister's difference, Hilary also felt a stubborn virgin pride. She didn't want ever to be undone out of her scepticism, or seduced into grown-up credulous susceptibility.

—But doesn't he think that we're poor, too? she asked fiercely. —Have you told him? Does he have any idea?

—It's different, said Sheila with finality. —It's just different.

When Hilary drove in the summer with her father in the Bedford van, to pick up Sheila and all her things at the end of her first year, she was waiting for them of course at Manor Hall, as if there had never been any other place, any squat whose kitchen was painted with giant mushrooms. Hilary understood that she was not ever to mention what had happened there, not even when she and Sheila were alone. Because they never wore the memory out by speaking of it, the place persisted vividly in her imagination.

She had stayed on in that house for almost a week: she had arrived on Monday and her return ticket was for Saturday. Sheila rested for the first couple of days, sleeping a lot, and Hilary went out on her own, exploring, going round the shops. On Sheila's instructions she took several carrier bags of bloody sheets and towels to the launderette, where she sat reading Virginia Woolf while the washing boiled. There seemed to be a lot of hours to pass, because she didn't want to spend too much time in Sheila's room; she shrank from the possibility of getting in the way between Sheila and Neil. A couple of times she went to the cinema in the afternoon by herself. They all went out to pubs every evening and she got used to drinking beer, although she didn't get to like it. While the others joked and drank and

smoked she sat in a silence that must have looked gawky
and immature, so that she was sure Sheila despaired of her,
although Sheila must also surely have known that she found
the conversation impossible to join because it was so tepid
and disappointing, gossip mostly about people she'd never
met. Sheila, who had been aloof and not popular at school,
seemed to be working hard to make these people like her.
She made herself brighter and funnier and smaller than her
real self, Hilary thought. She surrounded Neil in particular
with such efforts of admiration, prompting him and encouraging him and attributing ideas to him, while he smiled in
lazy amusement, rolling up his eternal cigarettes. At least
they weren't all over each other, they didn't cling together
in public. Hilary even feared for Neil, thinking that he
shouldn't trust her sister, he should wonder what dark
undertow might follow after such a glittering bright flood.

By the end of the week Sheila was well enough to go
to lectures again, and on the Saturday she came to the bus
station to see Hilary off. She insisted on carrying Hilary's
suitcase, which swung in her hand as light as if there was
nothing in it, now that their father's old dictionaries of clas-
sical mythology had been unloaded.

—I didn't feel anything, you know, Sheila said as they
walked, as if she was picking up on some discussion they
had only broken off a few moments before, although in
fact they hadn't talked once, since it was over, about what
had happened to her. —I mean, apart from physically. Just
like a tummy upset. That's all it was: a nuisance.

—All right, if you say so.

For the first time Sheila talked about her studies. She had
to write an essay on the *Oresteia* which she said was all
about the sex war, female avenging Furies and male reason.

—*The gods are disgusted at you*, she said gleefully. —Apollo
to the Furies. *Apoptustoi theosis. Never let your filth touch
anything in my sacred shrine.*

When Hilary was in her seat in the coach, Sheila stayed hanging around outside the window although Hilary signed to her to go, there was no need to wait. They laughed at one another through the glass, helpless to communicate: for the first time they were in tune together as they used to be. Sheila mouthed something and Hilary mimed elaborately: frowned, shook her head, shrugged her shoulders. She couldn't understand. Sheila put her face close to the glass and cupped her hands round her mouth, shouting. She was wearing a woollen knitted hat with knitted flowers pulled down over her ears.

—Give my love to everybody!

Hilary saw that all of a sudden her sister didn't want her to go. She was seized then by an impulse to struggle off the coach, to stay and fight, as if Sheila had after all been abducted by a Bluebeard: she felt focused as a crusader in her opposition to Neil. She even half turned round in her seat, as if to get out. But there was a man in the seat beside her, she would have had to ask him to move, he was settled behind his newspaper. The moment and the possibility passed. The coach reversed, the sisters waved frantically, and then Sheila was gone and Hilary subsided into her solitude, keeping her face averted from the man who had seen too much of her excitement, and whose newspaper anyway would make her sick if she accidentally read any of the headlines.

Above the city buildings the sky was blue and pale with light, drawn across by thin skeins of transparent cloud. Beyond the outskirts of the city everything was bursting with the spring growth which was further on over here than in the east. The tips of the hedgerows and the trees, if they hadn't yet come into leaf, gave off a red haze where the twigs swelled and shone. It seemed extraordinary to Hilary that her life must at some point soon change as completely and abruptly as Sheila's had, so that everything

familiar would be left behind. She sat with bubbles of excitement rising in her chest. The scruffy undistinguished countryside outside the coach window seemed to her beautiful.
It desolated her to think that when she was dead she
wouldn't be able to see it: cows, green hummocky fields,
suburban cottages of weathered brick, a country factory
with smashed windows, an excited spatter of birds thrown
up from a tree. Then she started to see these things as if
she was dead already, and they were persisting after her, and
she had been allowed back, and must take in everything
hungrily while she had the chance, every least tiny detail.

PHOSPHORESCENCE

The Cooley boys used to spend all their summers at the cottage in West Wales. They had a boat, so most of the time they were on the water, or playing cricket on the beach, or helping their mother who was restoring the cottage. For whole days that summer when Graham was thirteen she was up on the roof in shorts and T-shirt and old daps, reslating. Their father went off every day alone, to paint landscapes.

That summer, as usual, various friends and family came and went, either staying at the cottage or in the tiny primitive chalet at the other end of the meadow which Graham's mother had done up for overspill visitors. It was to the chalet that Claudia and her family came: the Cooleys didn't know them well, her husband was some sort of technician in Graham's father's lab at the university. Their children were too small to join in the Cooley boys' games.

At first Graham took no more notice of Claudia than of any of the others who swam in and out of focus on the far-off adult surface of his world. Then she started to pay him attention in an extraordinary way. Fourth of five brothers, he was surprised enough if any of his parents' friends even remembered what school he was at and how old he was. Claudia, this grown-up mother of three children, began to make a point of sitting next to him. When they all squeezed into the back of the old Dormobile van, or around the cottage table for lunch, or in the sitting room

63

in the evening for cards and Monopoly, she simply sat up against him and then let the weight of her leg lie against his. They had bare legs, usually: he was still young enough for shorts even on cool days, and it was at the time when women wore short skirts. She shaved her legs, brown legs (his mother didn't): he saw the stubble, felt it. Sometimes, after a while, almost imperceptibly, she began to press, just slightly press. It always could just have been accidentally.

Probably she was doing it for a long time before he even noticed: he was thirteen, sex had hardly occurred to him, not as a physical reality he could have in connection with other people. And even once he'd noticed, once he'd started excitedly, scaredly, to wait for her to choose her place, even then he couldn't be sure, not at first, that he wasn't just crazily making it all up.

And at this point he began to take notice of Claudia all the time, to hardly take notice of anything else. She was plump and blonde, pretty, untidy: he noticed that a button kept slipping undone on a blouse too tight across her bust, and that her clothes bought to be glamorous were crumpled because her children were always clambering over her. Struggling down to the beach with a toddler on one arm and beach bags slung across her shoulder, she kept turning over on a sandal with a leather thong between her toes, and he heard her swear – shit! – in an undertone. Once he heard her snap at her husband, when she was trying to read the paperback book she brought down every day to the beach, and the children interrupted her one after another to pee or for food or quarrels, —If I don't get to finish this bloody sentence I'll scream! Graham's parents never swore, he only knew those words from school and from his brothers.

Claudia was a perfectly competent adult. She brought down to the beach everything her family needed: costumes and towels and picnic and suntan oil and changing stuff for the baby and rackets and balls. She fed them and soothed them all. One of her little girls stepped on a jellyfish and howled for half an hour before she fell asleep on Claudia's lap, while Claudia sat stroking her sticky salty hair. But when Graham watched her playing badminton with his brothers – dazzling against the sea, grunting and racing and scooping up the shuttlecock in halter top and John Lennon peaked cap – he saw that she was still young, not his kind of young, but Tim's and Alex's. That must be why she was still crazy enough to be doing this thing to him. She couldn't have done it to Tim or Alex because with them it would have been real, she would have had to acknowledge what was going on, they would have known. With him it was so completely, completely outside possibility. It couldn't be happening.

On the beach it wasn't possible to be squeezed side by side. But she found other ways: he'd feel a gritty sandpapery toe just making contact, or when she reached across him to hand out sandwiches, he'd get a scorch of the flesh of her arm against his shoulder. It was so subtle that no one, however scrupulously they watched, could ever have seen: it was a chain of innocent accidents only connected through his burning consciousness of her touch.

On the surface she was particularly nice to him, asking him about school, asking his opinions on things the others talked about, the boat, the weather. She chose him to explain to her the rules of racing demon; he had to play through the first couple of hands with her. When she leaned excitedly forward over the table to see what had been played – she was short-sighted but wouldn't wear her glasses – she wedged him heavily into the corner, he smelled her sweat. His mother complimented Claudia on how she drew Graham out. He was supposed to be the shy one in the family arrangement: Alex was the brainy one, Phil the sporty one, and so on.

He began to be hardly able to look at his mother. She was like a humming black space where something familiar and unquestioned had previously been: he couldn't hold her and Claudia in his mind at the same time. Passionately he began to love all the things Claudia did differently to his mother: she yawned when his mother waxed indignant about conservation or bureaucracy, she opened tins for her family's supper (the chalet kitchen was primitive, but his mother would have done a slow-cooking casserole), she flirted with his father, leaning over him to see how the day's painting had gone. She smoked cigarettes. She wore lipstick and stuff on her eyes, she smelled of perfume, she confessed carelessly that she wouldn't know how to change a plug, let alone rewire a house (this was what Graham's mother had done in the cottage, the previous summer).

One night, the last of Claudia's family's stay, there was a very high tide: the whole flat sandy bottom of the valley they usually walked down to reach the beach was flooded with the sea. They made a bonfire, cooked sausages and potatoes, and took it in turns to take a rowing boat out on the water. It was shallow and calm; they had to watch out for the current where the river flowed, but his mother didn't believe in overprotecting them. The water that night was full of phosphorescence, tiny sea creatures that glowed in the dark: an enzyme-catalysed chemical reaction, their father told them.

Graham took Claudia out in the boat with her daughters: she sat opposite him while he rowed, and the two little girls cuddled on either side of her, hushed and still for once. Every time he lifted the oars out of the water they dripped with liquid light in the darkness, and where the oars dropped into the water they made bright holes and ripples of light went racing out from them. In the dark Claudia took her feet out of her shoes and put them on his. He was rowing in bare feet, he'd left his flip-flops on the sand. He rowed

66

up and down, his stroke faultless, in a kind of trance, until eventually the others were shouting for them from the shore.

—Come on, you idiot! Don't hog the boat! Give someone else a go!

And all the time she was rubbing her feet up and down his; he could feel the thick calloused skin on her heels and on the ball of her foot, her splayed brown toes and the hard polish of her nails, the sand she ground against him, that stuck to their ankles and calves in the wet bottom of the boat.

Then the next day she went, and he suffered. For the first time like an adult, secretly.

More than twenty-five years later, when Graham had children of his own, he saw Claudia again. The sixth-form college he taught at was sometimes hired out for functions out of school hours: one Friday when he'd had to stay late for a meeting, he met the delegates for some conference coming in as he left. His glance fell on the board in the foyer: a course on food hygiene. The woman who came up the front steps directly at him, her conference folder hugged across her chest, chatting with assurance to a friend, was stouter, and smarter (her buttons were all done up), and her hair was a shining even grey, cut in a shoulder-length bob. But it was unmistakably her: the pugnacious jaw, the upturned nose, the wide mouth. These things about her he'd forgotten for decades suddenly reconnected themselves into the unmistakable stamp of her.

The moment she had passed, he doubted it. He was hallucinating; some chance feature of a stranger had triggered a memory he hadn't known he'd kept. He turned and saw her disappearing through the double doors. Then another woman with a folder came running up the steps, looking past him: she'd seen someone she knew. Claudia! she called. And the grey-haired woman turned.

★

That night when his wife came in from seeing a film with her girlfriends, brash and defensive from her couple of drinks in the arts centre bar, he told her about Claudia. He had been sitting marking a pile of school folders; he saw her take in the mugs with black coffee dregs left on the desk as if they were reproachful reminders of how austerely dutiful he was. Of his puritanism, as she called it.

He wasn't sure why he told her about Claudia now. Carol had insisted years ago on confessing all her experiences with men, but he hadn't really wanted to know, not out of jealousy but real indifference: how could these things be shared? But she leaned across him to collect the mugs and he caught the blare of wine on her breath: he imagined that she'd been complaining about him as usual to Rose and Fran, that the only things he ever got excited about were quantum mechanics and quarks. Then he felt as if he had cheated her out of some knowledge of himself without which she was vulnerable.

He told her when they were lying in bed together in the dark. She didn't like his story. At first she didn't believe it. —Oh, but Gray! You were just fantasising! Why would a grown-up sensible woman want . . .

Then she got up and put on the light, sat down at the dressing table and creamed her face, briskly and matter-of-factly, as if she'd forgotten to do it before she came to bed, working cream in with her fingertips against the downwards droop, concentrating angrily on her reflection.

—But what would you think if you heard about this . . . If you heard about a man, doing this to a thirteen-year-old girl, to your own daughter, to Hannah, what would you think? It's *horrible*.

He didn't tell her that he'd seen Claudia again.

He found out her address quite easily, by telephoning the conference organisers. He went to the house twice in his

68

lunch hour when there was no one there. The house was tucked away down a little mews street, a square Georgian house with a modern glassy extension: when he peered inside he could see Turkish rugs on a stone-flagged floor, abstract paintings on the walls, a huge white paper globe for a lampshade. He checked the address on his piece of paper to be sure it was really hers: everything about the house was quietly wealthy, far beyond the reach of a laboratory technician, or even a university lecturer.

The third time he went after school and there was a plum-coloured old Jaguar parked in the courtyard under the flowering cherry, a few petals scattered on its bonnet. Claudia answered the door. She was dressed in a batik-printed kimono and he could smell the smoke from the cigarette she had just put down.

—Claudia? It's Graham Cooley.

She was perfectly blank, searched her memory half-heartedly, accepting the hand he put out.

—It's a long time ago. You came on holiday with us, stayed in our chalet in West Wales.

—Oh: Cooley! A long time ago! Goodness me! I do remember, I think. That family with all the boys. Which one were you? But that was in another lifetime! How extraordinary. And of course you're grown up.

She still didn't make that movement from the door which would invite him in: she was stubbornly guarding whatever little ritual of peace and privacy he had interrupted. Close to, he could see where the skin was loosening to hang under her jaw, and the eyes sun-crinkled from too many tans.

He insisted. With obvious misgivings – what ever did he want? – and finding it difficult even to remember anything about his mother and father to make conversation out of, she let him in and made him coffee and sat him in the glass room in a chair made of blond wood and tubular chrome opposite hers. The coffee was good, strong espresso.

—So what have you done with yourself then, Graham? she said. You were an awfully talented family, weren't you? Terrifying. What about your brothers? Were you the third? Tim, wasn't it, and Paul?

—Not Paul, he said, Philip. I was the fourth. He reached across – the chrome chair, although it looked awkward, was comfortable and supportive – and put his hand heavily on her leg above the knee. She had put on a lot of weight, was really very solid between bust and hips, but her flesh was compact and warm. —Don't you remember? Really?

She froze. She looked at him in horror, at first only thinking, whoever is he, how to get him out of here, why ever did I let him in, against my better judgement? But then as he searched her eyes something behind them burst, some containing membrane, and what she remembered spread through her, filling her, making her skin flush deeper and deeper, making her body sag and yield, filling her eyes with water even. —Oh, yes, she said. Oh . . . Oh, so you did know. Oh, God, I'd managed to convince myself afterwards that you wouldn't have noticed, that it had just been my own fantasy . . . And then, just now, I simply forgot, I'd forgotten all about it, it's years since I've thought about that summer . . .

—You do remember?

—Well, something awful. I really thought, though, you wouldn't have guessed, that it was all just my own horrible idea.

—But in the boat . . .

—In the boat? In the boat? What did I do in the boat? Oh, don't tell me, please, I don't want to know. God – I can't explain it, there's no explanation. When my own son got to that age I used to think, that boy . . . It was such a rotten summer, Don and I . . . I remember I used to sit there on the beach just dreaming of lacerating him all over with a kitchen knife. Poor Don. He really wasn't so bad. Cooped up all summer together in that awful hut. She looked at him with shock. —You do know that Don and I split up? No, of course, why should you? But that was in another lifetime, really. My husband's an architect. We had another daughter together, four children altogether . . . She spelled out these things as if she owed him explanations.

—Are the children at school?

—At school? Her eyes were wet again, her loose mouth slipped, smiling, she took his hand off her knee. —I'm a grandmother. I've got two grandchildren. The daughter you didn't know – she's at art college, final year. You see – I'm an old woman. Hideous, isn't it? Oh God, this is awful. Let's have a drink.

She poured them both huge splashes of Scotch.

—But your name's the same, that's how I followed you up.

—I didn't want all that business, taking my husband's name. I wanted to do things differently, the second time. Whether it worked out so very different, this man–woman thing, it's so difficult . . . They chinked glasses, she blushed very darkly. —Have you forgiven me? It hasn't ruined your life or anything? I'm really so ashamed. I was, afterwards; then I began to wonder if I really could have done anything so awful. I thought I might have just dreamed it. But of course I've never thought I'd see you, that we'd recognise one another. We lived in the north for years.

—I recognised you. Why food hygiene, by the way?

She was blank again. —Oh! Food hygiene! She ran mentally over a room of faces. —Were you at that conference? Yes – I part own a restauraunt, a French restaurant in Kingsmile.

They drank their whisky quickly and she poured more with shaking hands. She looked appeasingly into his face. —You are nice-looking, she said. —I always had good taste in men. Oh dear. It is all right, isn't it? You haven't come to punish me or anything?

—No, he said. —That's the last thing.

Nonetheless, when he began kissing her and putting his hands under her clothes, he did it without tentativeness, as if he was claiming something he was owed. And she let him, watched him, said, —Are you really sure? I don't think of anyone wanting this from me any more. I mean, any stranger.

—I'm not a stranger, he said.

—You are to me. In spite of everything you tell me. I remember it, just. But of course not with you. I remember a boy, you see. I've never seen you before.

But she didn't stop him. Several times, for all his intentness, he caught her look of curiosity at him, curiosity like his own, hard and greedy and tinged with shame.

Carol swung the door open as he put his key in the lock.

—Where have you been? I've been out of my mind. I've phoned all the hospitals, your dinner's ruined, the kids –

—Carol, didn't I tell you? We had a GCSE moderation, it went on for bloody hours. I'm sure I told you. I said I'd get sandwiches.

—But I phoned the college, there was no answer.

—Love, I'm sorry . . . The phone rings in the office, there's no one there to pick it up. I'm sorry, maybe I did forget to mention it. I was so sure I had. Let me come in and get the kids to bed for you.

She stood staring at him. —It's so unlike you. You're usually so organised. But I really don't remember you telling me about this one. And isn't it a bit early for a moderation? You haven't finished marking all the papers yet.

For a moment he was sure she could smell something on him, see something of the dazzle that was clinging to him, dripping off him, flashing round in his veins. But he saw her deliberately tidy that intimation away, out of consciousness. This was her husband, the man she knew. He was a physics teacher and competition-standard chess player, wasn't he?

THE ENEMY

When Keith had finished up the second bottle of wine he began to yawn, the conversation faltered companionably as it can between old friends, and then he took himself off to bed in Caro's spare room, where she knew he fell asleep at once between her clean white sheets because she heard him snort or snuffle once or twice as she was carrying dishes past the door. She relished the thought of his rather ravaged fifty-five-year-old and oh-so-male head against her broderie anglaise pillowcases. Caro herself felt awake, wide awake, the kind of awakeness that seizes you in the early hours and brings such ultimate penetration and clarity that you cannot imagine you will ever sleep again. She cleared the table in the living room where they had eaten together, stacked the dishes in the dishwasher ready to turn on in the morning, washed up a few delicate bowls and glasses she didn't trust in the machine, tidied the kitchen. In her bare feet she prowled around the flat, not able to make up her mind to undress and go to bed. Tomorrow was Sunday, she didn't have to get up for work.

What was it about Keith, after all this time, that could still make her restless; could make her feel this need to be vigilant while he snored? When they sat eating and drinking together she hadn't felt it; she had felt fond of him, and that his old power to stir and upset her was diminished. He was nicer than he used to be, no doubt about that. They had talked a lot about his children; the ones he had

had with Penny, Caro's sister, who were in their twenties now, and then the younger ones he had with his second wife Lynne. She had been amused that he – who had once been going to 'smash capitalism' – took a serious and know-ledgeable interest in the wine he had brought with him for them to drink (he had come to her straight from France; he and Lynne seemed to spend most of the year at their farmhouse in the Dordogne).

Nonetheless the thought came involuntarily into her head as she prowled, that tonight she had her enemy sleeping under her roof. Of all things: as if instead of a respectable middle-aged PA living in suburban Cardiff she was some kind of Anglo-Saxon thane, sharpening her sword and thinking of blood. Just as the thane might have, she felt divided between an anxious hostility towards her guest and an absolute requirement to protect him and watch over his head.

In May 1968 Caro had turned up for a meeting of the Revolutionary Socialist Student Federation at her university wearing a new trouser suit: green corduroy bell-bottoms with a flower-patterned jacket lining and Sergeant Pepper-style military buttons. The meeting was to organise participation in a revolutionary festival in London the following month, generating support for the Vietnamese struggle for national liberation. The festival was already provoking all kinds of ideological dissent: the Trotskyists thought the whole project was 'reformist', and the Communist Party were nervous at the use of the word 'revolutionary'. The Young Communists were going to appear riding a fleet of white bicycles which they had collected and were donating to the Vietnamese.

Caro had bought the trouser suit because her godmother (whom she had adored as a little girl but had stopped visiting recently because of her views on trade unions and immi-gration) had sent her twenty-one pounds for her twenty-first birthday. She could have put it aside to help eke out the end of her grant, but instead, on impulse, she had gone shopping and spent it in a trendy boutique in town that she had never dared to go inside before. It was months since she had had any new clothes; and she had never possessed anything quite so joyous, so up to the minute and striking, as this trouser suit. She knew that it expressed perfectly on the outside the person she wanted to be from within. With her long hair and tall lean figure it made her look sexy, defiant, capable (in skirts she often only looked gawky and mannish).

The meeting was in a basement room in the History Department as usual. As usual, it was mostly men, though there were three or four girls, bright history and politics students, friends of Caro's, who came regularly. The girls really did get asked to make the tea, and really did make it. They sat at desks arranged in a square under a bleak light bulb with an institutional-type glass shade, surrounded by maps on the walls that were of course nothing to do with them – Europe after the Congress of Vienna, the Austro-Hungarian Empire in 1914 – but nonetheless gave the place an air they all rather enjoyed of being a command centre in some essential world-changing operation. By the time Caro arrived the usual thick fug of cigarette smoke was already building up (she smoked too, in those days). She was greeted, because of the trouser suit, with a couple of wolf whistles, and everyone looked up. It was complicated to remember truthfully now just how one had felt about that whistling. A decade later it became obligatory for women to be indignant at it and find it degrading; at the time, however, she would probably have felt without it that her trouser suit had failed of its effect. You met the whistle without making eye contact but with a little warm curl of an acknowledging smile, a gleam of response.

Two men had come from Agit Prop, to talk to the meeting

about the festival (Agit Prop was a loose association of activists and artists named after Trotsky's propaganda train and dedicated to promoting revolutionary messages through aesthetic means). That was how Caro met Keith Reid for the first time: when she arrived he had already taken his place in a chair at the centre of things, commanding the whole room. Keith was a very attractive man – it was the first thing you needed to know about him, to get any idea of who he was, then. Not handsome, exactly: off-centre quirky features held together by a fluid energy, fragile hooked nose, hollow cheeks, a lean loose strong body, a shoulder-length mess of slightly greasy dark curls. He had a Welsh accent: it was a Valleys accent in fact – he was from Cwmbach near Aberdare – but in those days Caro had never been to Wales and couldn't tell one accent from another. At a time when Left politics was saturated in the romance of the workers, this accent was in itself enough to melt most of the women (and the men).

He looked at Caro in her trouser suit.

—Don't you find, he said, —that dressing up like that puts off the working classes?

She thought about this now with stupefaction. Had she really once inhabited a world where such absurdities were a currency? She should have laughed in his face. She should have turned round and walked out of the meeting and never gone back.

—No, she said, calmly taking a place directly in Keith's line of sight, so that he could get his eyeful of the offending item, —I find it gives them something good to look at.

Of course she wasn't really calm. She was raging, and humiliated, and struggling with a muddled and not yet confident sense of something fundamentally flawed and unfair to do with men and women in what he had said and all that lay behind it: everything that was going over-flow into the flood of feminism in the next couple of decades. And no doubt at the same time she was scalding with shame at her bourgeois depraved frivolity in the face of decent suffering working-class sobriety, just as Keith meant her to be. And she was thinking how she would make him pay for that.

They had such energy, then, for all the battles.

After the meeting the visitors from Agit Prop had needed a floor to stay on and Caro had taken them back to the disintegrating old mock-Tudor house, its garden overgrown as a jungle, which she shared with a motley collection of students and friends and politicos. (Later she had had trouble with that house; it was rented in her name, and some of the people using it refused to pay their share. She had to hassle them for it, and came home once to find 'Rachman bitch' scrawled in red paint on her bedroom wall.) They sat up until late smoking pot and sparring; Caro and Keith arguing not about the trouser suit, which wasn't mentioned again, but about the dockers' support for Enoch Powell and its implications for the alliance between left alternative politics and the working-class movement. Caro had been on the anti-racist march to Transport House: Keith thought she was overstating the problem in a way that was typical of bourgeois squeamishness in the face of the realities of working-class culture.

The way Keith dominated a room and laid down the law and didn't seriously countenance anybody else's opinions should have made him obnoxious; but his ironic delivery in that accent of his made it seem as though there was something teasing in his most exaggerated assertions. Everyone was willing to listen to him because he was older and his pedigree was impeccable: a miner's son, kicked out of Hornsey Art College for his political activities, he had been working on building sites ever since. In any case, that sheer imperturbable male certainty was intriguing to women in those days. They felt in the face of it a complex mix of thrilled abjection with a desire to batter at it with their fists; also, probably strongest, they believed that given the chance they would be able to find out through their feminine sexuality the weaknesses and vulnerable places behind the imperturbable male front. (This last intuition was all too often accurate.)

Eventually Caro found sleeping bags for everybody and they distributed themselves around mattresses and sofas and floors in the high-ceilinged damp-smelling rooms of the house. And then at some point in the night Keith must have got up again and wandered about until he found, not Caro, who had half expected him, but her sister Penny, who happened to be staying with her for a few days. Penny was a year older than Caro but didn't look it: most people took her to be the younger sister. She was smaller, softer-seeming, prettier. Caro found them in the morning twined around one another in their zipped-together sleeping bags. All she could make out at first was the mess of Keith's dark curls and his naked young shoulders, tanned and muscular from the work he did; and then she saw how down inside the bag Penny's head with its swirl of auburn hair like a fox's brush was wrapped in his brown arms against his chest.

She remembered that she had felt a stinging shock. Not heartbreak or any kind of serious sorrow: she hadn't had time to do anything like fall in love with Keith, and anyway, love didn't seem to be quite what it was that could have happened, if things had gone differently, between them. It was more as if she felt that, if you put the two of them alongside Keith Reid, it was in some obvious way she and not Penny who was his match, his mate. Penny all through the loud debate of the night before had sat quietly while Caro met him, point for point, and smoked joint for joint with him. Also, there was unfinished business between her and him: some contest he had begun and had now abruptly – it made him seem almost cowardly – broken off. Even as Caro recoiled, just for that first moment, in the shock of finding them, she knew she was learning from it something essential she needed to know for her survival, something about the way that men chose women.

Penny had given up after one year at art college and was living at home again with their parents in Banbury. She was thinking about going to do teacher training. Instead, she embarked on the relationship with Keith: it did almost seem, in retrospect, like a career choice. That whole long middle section of Penny's life, twenty years, was taken up in the struggle with him: pursued by him; dedicating herself to him; counselling him through his creative agonies when he was writing; bearing his children; supporting his infidelities, his drinking, his disappearances, his contempts; making every effort to tame him, to turn him into a decent acceptable partner and father. Then when Penny had finished with him once and for all, he slipped without a protest into cosy domesticity with his second wife, as if there hadn't ever been a problem. —I was just the warm-up act, Penny joked about it now. —Softening him up ready for the show with Lynne.

Through all of it, Caro had supported her sister: sometimes literally, with money, mostly just with listening and company and sympathy. When Keith went back to live in Wales and got Welsh Arts Council funding to make the first film, Penny had two small babies. Instead of finding a house in Cardiff, even in Pontypridd, Keith had insisted – on principle – on taking her to live in a council house on the edge of a huge bleak estate on the side of a mountain in Merthyr Tydfil where she didn't know anyone, and no one liked her because she was posh and English. It was half an hour's walk with the pushchair down to the nearest shops. When a job came up in Cardiff, Caro moved there partly to be near enough to help (she was also escaping the fag end of a tormenting love affair): most weekends after work she drove up to Merthyr to give a hand with the kids, take Penny to the nearest supermarket, and try to persuade her to pack up her things and leave. Penny had made the house inside gorgeous on next to nothing, with rush mats and big embroidered cushions and mobiles and chimes pinned to the ceiling; she painted the lids of instant coffee jars in rainbow colours and kept brown rice and lentils and dried kidney beans in them. But the wind seemed never to stop whistling around the corners of the house and in through the ill-fitting window frames, setting the mobiles swinging.

Keith usually wasn't there and if he was he and Caro hardly spoke. One strange Saturday evening he had had a gun for some reason: perhaps it was to do with the film, she couldn't remember, although that wouldn't have explained why he also had live ammunition. He had claimed that he knew how to dismantle it, had taken bits off it and spread them out on the tablecloth in the corner of the room where the children were watching television: he was drinking whisky, and erupted with raucous contempt when Penny said she didn't want that horrible thing in her home. He picked the gun up and held it to Penny's head while she struggled away from him and told him not to be so silly.

—Don't be such a bloody idiot, Keith, Caro said.

—Shut it, sister-bitch, he said in a fake cockney accent, swinging round, squinting his eyes, pretending to take aim at her across the room. Presumably without its bits the gun wasn't dangerous, but they couldn't be sure. They hurried the protesting children upstairs improbably early, bathed them with shaking hands, singing and playing games so as not to frighten them, staring at one another in mute communication of their predicament.

—Put the kids in the car and drive to my place, Caro

said, wrapping a towel around her wriggling wet niece, kissing the dark curls which were just like Keith's.

—Wait and see, said Penny, —if it gets any worse.

In the end Keith had not been able to put the gun back together, and had fallen asleep in front of the television: Penny hid the ammunition in her Tampax box before she went to bed. She had been right not to overreact: Keith wasn't really the kind of man who fired guns and shot people, he was the kind who liked the glamour of the idea of doing it.

Caro could remember going to see Keith's film at the arts centre in Cardiff – not at the premiere, she hadn't wanted to see him feted and basking in it, and had made her excuses, but in the week after – and it had made her so angry that she had wanted to stand up in the cinema and explain to all those admiring people in the audience how unforgivably he used real things that mattered and milked them to make them touching, and how in truth whenever he was home on the estate that he made so much of in the film he was bored and longing to get away to talk with his film-making friends. Actually the audience probably weren't really all that admiring, the film had got mixed reviews. She had seen it again recently when the arts centre did a Welsh film season, and had thought about it differently: only twenty years on it seemed innocent and archaic, and its stern establishing shots of pithead and winding gear were a nostalgic evocation of a lost landscape. The one he did afterwards about the miners' strike was his best, she thought: it was the bleakest most unsentimental account she ever saw of the whole business, capturing its honour and its errors both together; the ensemble work was very funny and complex (apart from the leads he had used non-professional actors, mostly ex-miners and their wives). His career had neither failed nor taken off, since then: there always seemed to be work, but it was always precarious (it was a good job Lynne made money with her photography).

In the end Penny made friends with some of the women from the estate she met in the school playground, and got involved with the tenants' association, and had her third baby in Prince Charles Hospital in Merthyr, and probably looked back now on her time on the estate with some affection. She grew very close, too, to Keith's parents in Cwmbach: she saw more of his father in his last illness than Keith did, she really seemed to love the reticent, neat old man, who had been an electrician at the Phurnacite plant and in his retirement pottered about his DIY tasks in their immaculate big post-war council house, putting a heated towel rail in the bathroom, making a patio for the garden. She stayed good friends with his mother and his sister even after she and Keith were separated.

When Penny eventually decided that he and she should go their different ways (she moved out when he tried to move his latest girlfriend, an actress with a drug habit and a dog, into the house with them), she did the teacher training she had put off for so long, and met her present partner, a biologist working in conservation who was everything suitable and reasonable that Keith was not. They lived now in the country near Banbury, not far from where Penny and Caro had grown up. Meanwhile Keith met Lynne, and they shared their time between London and the Dordogne. So that in the end it was Caro who was left living in Wales, and if she thought sometimes that it was partly because of Keith Reid that she had ended up making her life there she didn't mind, she just thought that it was funny.

She turned out all the lights in the flat; she could see well enough in the light that came from the street lamp outside her front window to pour herself a whisky in hopes that it would help put her to sleep. She sat to drink it with her feet tucked under her on the end of the sofa where she had sat an hour or so before listening to Keith; she heard a soft pattering of rain and a police siren, too far off to think about. In the half-dark, awareness of the familiar fond shapes of the furniture of her present life – tasteful and feminine and comfortable – was like a soft blanket settled around her shoulders. She should have felt safe and complete; it annoyed her that she was still gnawed by some unfinished business just because Keith Reid was asleep in her spare room. There were other men who had been much more important in her life, and yet when they came to stay (sometimes in the spare-room bed and sometimes in hers), it didn't bother her this way.

Her heart had sunk when halfway down the second bottle Keith began to wax nostalgic and maudlin about the sixties and the decay of the socialist dream. You heard this everywhere these days, in the newspapers and on television; usually of course from people who had been young then. The formula, surely inadequate to the complicated facts, was always the same: that what had been 'idealism' then had declined sadly into 'disillusion' now.

—But remember, she had insisted, —that in 1968 when we marched round Trafalgar Square we were chanting 'Ho Ho Ho Chi Minh'! I mean, for Chrissake! Ho Chi Minh! And at that revolutionary festival you could play skittles with French riot police helmets stuck on Coca-Cola bottles. And remember us getting up at the crack of dawn to go and try and sell *Socialist Worker* to workers in that clothing factory in Shacklewell Lane. Expecting them to spend their hard-earned money on that rag with its dreary doctrine and all its factional infighting. And I used to go back to bed afterwards, when I got home, because I hated getting up so early. Remember that we spoke with respect of Lenin, and Trotsky, and Chairman Mao, all those mass murderers.

Remember that we had contempt for the welfare state, as a piece of bourgeois revisionism.

—There were excesses, Keith conceded fondly. —But then, excess was in the air. Anything could have happened. That's what's missing now. Caro, you sound so New Labour. I'm still a revolutionary, aren't you? Don't you still want socialism?

She shrugged. —Oh, well, yes, socialism, I suppose . . .

That conversation had ended awkwardly, each embarrassed by what they thought of as the other's false position. Keith probably thought that Caro had 'sold out' (he might even have put it in those words, perhaps to Lynne). She worked as personal assistant to a Labour MP, a man she mostly liked and respected. (Before that she had worked for Panasonic.) On the second and fourth Mondays of every month she went to Amnesty International meetings in a shabby upstairs room of the Friends' Meeting House, and was currently involved in a campaign for the release of a postgraduate student imprisoned in China for his researches into ethnic Uighur history. This compromising pragmatic liberalism might in time turn out to be as absolutely beside the point as the articles she had once written for *Black Dwarf*: who could tell? Your ethical life was a shallow bowl brimming impossibly; however dedicatedly you carried it about with you there were bound to be spills, or you found out that the dedication you brought wasn't needed, or that you had brought it to the wrong place.

While Caro was tidying up she had had to go into the spare room to put away her grandmother's 1920s water jug, painted with blue irises, in its place on the lace mat on top of the bureau. This could have waited until the morning when Keith was gone; perhaps she had just made it an excuse to go in and take the measure of him uninhibitedly, free of the wakeful obligation to smile and reassure. She swung the door quietly behind her to admit just a narrow ribbon of light, then stood waiting for her eyes to adjust, breathing in the slight, not unpleasant fug of his smell: good French soap and cologne and a tang of his sweat and of gas flavoured with the garlic she had put in her cooking. He slept on his side with his face pressed in the pillow, frowning; his chest with its plume of grey-black hair down the breastbone was bare, the duvet lay decorously across his waist, under it he seemed to have his hands squeezed between his jackknifed knees, his mouth was open, he made noises sucking in air. She wondered all the time she stood there whether he wasn't actually aware of her presence and faking sleep.

He didn't look too bad. He took good care of himself (or Lynne took care of him): he hadn't put on much weight, although where he had been lean and hard he was nowadays rangy and slack, with jutting bowed shoulders under his T-shirt and a small soft pouch of belly above his belt. He probably still had the power of his sexual attraction; whereas Caro who was a couple of years younger knew she could no longer count on hers, even though she also took care of herself, and was slim, and had her hair coloured at Vidal Sassoon (she thought now that this old gender inequity probably had less to do with patriarchal systems than with desires hard-wired into human evolutionary biology). Keith had opted to deal with his advancing baldness by cutting very short even the rim of hair he had left growing behind his ears and at the back; this was a good move, she thought, pre-empting pretence and turning what might have looked like a vulnerability into an assertion of style. However, it made the starkness of his craggy head shocking. All the years of his age, all the drinking, all the history and difficulty of the man, was concentrated in the face laid bare: its eaten-out hollows, the high exposed bony bridge of his nose that rode him like the prow of his ship, the deep closed folds of flesh, the huge dropped purple eyelids flickering with sensitivity.

She sat thinking now about the time when Keith was the most attractive man in the room, the man you couldn't afford to turn your eyes away from, careless and dangerous with his young strength. It hadn't been a good or tender thing exactly; it hadn't had much joy in it for Caro. Nonetheless she quaked at the power of this enemy, stronger than either of them, who had slipped in under her roof and was stealing everything away.

When Keith had telephoned from France to say that he had to come over for a couple of days to talk to some people in Cardiff about a new film project, Caro had planned and shopped for an elaborate meal. She didn't make anything heavy or indigestible, but unusual things that took careful preparation, little Russian cheese pastries for starters, then fillet of lamb with dried maraschino cherries and spinach, and for dessert gooseberry sorbet with home-made almond tuiles. Because she lived alone, she loved to cook when she was entertaining friends.

She had spent all day getting ready what they had eaten in an hour or so. And of course the food had taken second place to their talk, with so much to catch up on; although Keith had helped himself hungrily and appreciatively. In her thirties she had resented furiously this disproportion between the time spent cooking and eating; it had seemed to her characteristic of women's work, exploitative and invisible and without lasting results. She had even given up cooking for a while. These days she felt about it differently. The disproportion seemed part of the right rhythm of all pleasure: a long, difficult and testing preparation for a few moments' consummation.

Now she used her mother's rolling pin to roll out her pastry; she kept Keith's mother's recipes for Welsh cakes and bara brith. In her tasks around the flat – polishing furniture, bleaching dishcloths, vacuuming, taking cuttings from her geraniums, ironing towels and putting them away in the airing cupboard – she was aware that her mother and grandmother had done these same things before her, working alone in quiet rooms, or with the radio for company. In truth she had had a stormy relationship with her parents, and used to think of her mother's domesticated life as thwarted and wasted. But she had learned to love the invisible work, the life that fell away and left no traces. This was how change happened, always obliquely to the plans you laid for it, leaving behind as dead husks all the preparations that you nonetheless had to make in order to bring it about.

THE SURROGATE

When I was twenty, not all that long ago, I fell in love with one of my lecturers at college. I know this is a very ordinary thing to do. And I know now that the lecturers sigh and feel anxious at the news of yet another smitten girl-child traipsing round moonily after them. They feel anxious and all those other things you would expect, too: flattered and confirmed and a bit stimulated.

His name was Patrick Hammett, and he taught Shake-speare and seventeenth-century poetry and critical theory. I chose all his courses; I made him my interpreter of the whole world. Patrick was tall, with rather bowed shoulders; he was hollowly thin except for a small beer belly nestled in the stretched cloth of his T-shirt above his belt. He wore his thick black hair down to his shoulders, tucked behind his ears. He used gold-rimmed glasses to read but took them off when he was talking and swung them in his fingers, and sometimes dropped them; his eyes without the glasses were deep-set and squinted slightly. In a crowd, in a club, you wouldn't have picked him out as particularly good-looking. But in the lecture room, sitting with us in the democratic circle of chairs that he insisted upon, his looks were a power, a force that I felt physically, like velvet against my skin. I loved the whitened pressure points that his glasses left on the bridge of his thin nose. I loved the big nervous hands he was always waving in the air, gesturing uncontrollably in accompaniment to his words.

Of course I didn't have a chance with him. Who was I? I wasn't anybody. I wasn't even one of the cleverest in the classes. I wasn't an absolutely average student either; I was aware that I had a quirky way of looking at things, which sometimes came out as insight and sometimes just left everyone looking blank. Patrick encouraged me. Once, he reminded all of them of something I'd said. —You remember the point that Carla made in last week's seminar? Another time, after I'd made some remark about freedom of choice in *Much Ado About Nothing*, he said, —That's very well expressed, Carla. I couldn't have put that more eloquently myself. This made me very happy. But I didn't delude myself. I wasn't the kind of student who would get a first-class mark. When I tried to put my thoughts down in writing, the dart of intuition that was clear and sharp when it flew into my mind got tangled in something muffling and clumsy. And Patrick's being surprised sometimes by my penetration didn't really mean he had singled me out. I didn't really exist for him, outside that circle of chairs in the lecture room.

In the seventeenth-century poetry seminar he read us 'An Exequy', by Henry King.

> *Dear loss! Since thy untimely fate*
> *My task hath been to meditate*
> *On thee, on thee: thou art the book,*
> *The library whereon I look*
> *Though almost blind . . .*
> *   'Tis true, with shame and grief I yield,*
> *Thou like the Van first took'st the field,*
> *And gotten hast the victory*
> *In thus adventuring to dy*
> *Before me, whose more years might crave*
> *A just precedence in the grave.*
> *But heark! My Pulse like a soft Drum*

> *Beats my approach, tells* Thee *I come;*
> *And slow howere my marches be,*
> *I shall at last sit down by* Thee.

I can't adequately express the effect this poem had on me then. I don't remember now what season of the year it was, but I do remember that we had the strip lights on in the lecture room in the middle of the day because the sky was so dark outside, navy-blue clouds pressing close to the earth like an artificial ceiling. Little gouts of rain were spitting against the window, and in the gently sloping field outside (the campus was built up around an eighteenth-century house in the middle of an estate farmed by the Duchy of Cornwall) the bullocks, instead of lying down as they should have done with rain coming, were jostling uneasily and heaving up against the fence and clambering on to one another's backs.

When I look at the poem now, I see that it is the lament of a much older man for a young wife snatched away by death, and that it depends upon a confidence in the resurrection of the body on Judgement Day. I don't know anything about those things. But at the time I felt that the words of the poem were so immediate and relevant that they spoke to me not just through my mind but through my body. I could hear that Drum; its beating came right up out of the floor of the classroom and shook me through the soles of my feet. I made one of those remarks that didn't come out well, and nobody took much notice of it. —He longs for her and she isn't there, I said. It sounded too obvious to need stating. I'd wanted to use the word 'sexual' (we were trained to see sexual implications everywhere, and surely in this case I would have been right), but I couldn't bring myself to be the first to say it. Patrick wanted us to talk about the metaphor of the beloved object as text ('thou art the book, / The library whereon I look'). For me the

poem was Patrick. All its passion, its concentration, I attrib-
uted to him. The poem became my intimation of the pulse
of his life, from which I was shut out.

He was only seven or eight years older than we were,
but we thought his life must be made out of different stuff
to the lives we knew. As far as we could tell he wasn't
married or living with anyone. Someone said he had once
had a relationship with a student (although they're not
supposed to). That didn't make me any more hopeful. She
had probably been one of the clever ones who got firsts.
She had probably been beautiful. I didn't think I was. My
looks (I'm small and blonde with eyes that used to make
the kids at school call me frogface) were like the quirky
things I said in class. Good on a good day.

I dreamed about him all the time. I don't mean sleeping
dreams, although sometimes he was in those as well. Too
many of my waking hours were spent fantasising scenes in
which Patrick and I somehow met outside the classroom
and our relationship was changed out of distant acquain-
tance into passionate *amour*. I was very exacting as the author
and director of these scenes in my mind. Nothing must
happen in them that was absurdly improbable or out of
character. Patrick wasn't ever allowed, for example, to tell
me that he had always loved me, that he had been fascinated by me from the moment I first walked into the lecture
room. The scene could begin with no more than a friendly
appreciation of an interested student, a teacherly investment
in my intellectual development. He might at most be
allowed a little stir of vanity at the depth and earnestness
of my response to him.

Given these constraints, the journey from the plausible
encounter to the moment when he reached out for me
could still be travelled in a thousand different ways. (Even
in my fantasies I didn't dare reach out for him, in case he

turned me down.) He had to be surprised out of his position of friendly neutrality and into a dawning, uneasy recognition of his growing attraction to me, an attraction that he perhaps couldn't quite rationally account for. The transformation could be precipitated in various ways; these were the only extravagance I allowed myself. Sometimes we would be accidentally stranded by a breakdown in the middle of nowhere, after he'd innocently offered me a lift home from college. Or we'd be caught by a freak storm when calling at a cottage belonging to friends of his to pick up some books he'd lent them. Or he would have to take refuge in my room one night after being beaten up by muggers and left bleeding in the road just as I was on my way home.

My favourite scene was acted out somewhere that I don't think I've ever actually been. I imagined a path through a green meadow. I'm absolutely a city girl and don't know much about the countryside but of course I've visited it. I needed to be clear in my mind exactly how we'd got there. Sometimes it was in the aftermath of some other encounter nearer home. ('Why don't you come out for a walk next weekend, and I'll show you where Coleridge is supposed to have started writing "The Ancient Mariner"?') Or a whole group of us were out on a college field trip and Patrick and I got separated from the others while we were talking. (Tricky, as the only trip he ever came on was to the theatre at Stratford.) Or he had employed me to do some research over the holidays and then on impulse said he'd like to buy me tea in the country as a reward.

We'd walk down this grassy path and reach a gate, which opened into a wood beyond. At the threshold of the wood the light changed from broad bright sunlight to a secretive and dappled shade. There were rustlings among the dead leaves that spread like a carpet under the trees. It was a place I'd invented for a transition, for the passage over from my life into his, from his to mine. The gate was made of old grey wood washed silvery by the rain, it swung crookedly on rusting hinges. He held it open for me, or I climbed over and he helped me down. Something in the change of light stilled us, made us pause; the wood with its pillar-like tree trunks and its tracery of branches was a cathedral. He was still supporting my weight, or I was cast up against him in some way as I came through the gate or passed him on the narrow path. I could feel the heat of his body under the ragged grey wool of the sweater he really often wore.

I could only really sustain the stories up to this point. After that, his face came closer, he put his arms around me, there was kissing, there was pressing together, and the narrative failed; it lost its sequence. I could – and did – imagine plenty of what happened after, but not in a clear order. It came in a hallucinated muddle. I would try to disentangle it. I'd return again and again to the gate, the threshold, the movement with which he reached across the distance between us. I'd start again from there. But it was no good. The dream beyond that point was a stuck film repeating itself. Exhausting, after a while. Dispiriting. Because in truth it was nothing at all.

In my second year I was so short of money that I got a job working three evenings a week at a pub in town. It must have been an old pub once, with lots of twisty little rooms winding around the different levels, but it had been knocked through into one huge, cavernous space, low-ceilinged and gloomy. There were still confusing steps up and down in places, and the floor changed from flagstones to boards to carpets; drunks and women in heels sometimes tripped and spilled their beer. Games machines flashing ruby- and emerald-coloured lights stood against the walls. The place didn't have much atmosphere. It was more fashionable to go to one of the new bars with long pine tables and stainless-steel counters, where food was served; or to one of the old quaint pubs that had kept their little rooms and served real ale. Big parties came to my pub because there was usually room to seat them all. And men came in to watch the football on the TV screens; the kind of men who didn't want roasted vegetables in pittas or real ale.

I'd worked in nicer pubs. When I lived at home I'd worked in our local, where the old-timers expected you to start pulling their pints the moment they pushed open the door. I didn't mind the anonymity of this place. I was often on with temporary staff I didn't know, and that meant I didn't have to talk too much. If we weren't busy, I just kept order behind the bar. I made sure that the glasses were clean, the lemons sliced, the drip trays emptied, the bottles in the optics replaced as soon as they ran out, the ice bucket filled.

While I was taking care of all this I forgot that I was a student. I rarely saw anyone from the college in there, students or staff. Then one night when I came back from asking the landlord to change a barrel, I thought for a moment that I saw Patrick. A man with the same long narrow build and thick shoulder-length hair was standing with his back to the bar, a pint of lager in one hand, looking up at the TV screen. Although this was exactly the sort of plausible scenario I was always dreaming up to bring us together, in reality I didn't want it to be him. I panicked. I didn't think I could cope with my two roles at once – competent barmaid and besotted student – and I had no idea how to respond when he turned round and recognised me. But the man, when he turned round, wasn't Patrick, though he did look rather like him. Rather like him but quite different. He had the same crooked nose – more exaggerated, even – and the same close-together eyes that you saw when Patrick took his glasses off. But he didn't wear glasses. He didn't have any of Patrick's concentrated excitement.

He asked for a pint of Stella in an ordinary accent, not like Patrick's educated one. When I smiled at him and made some comment about the match, he blushed, and I guessed that he was shy, and maybe not very clever. He probably would have liked to keep the conversation going, but he couldn't think of what to say to me. And I got a certain pleasure out of the situation. It was like a game; I could play at talking to Patrick, without its really mattering, without being afraid of what he thought of what I said. I chatted while I was handing his change over, before I was called away to serve someone else. When he left the pub, fifteen minutes later, he put his glass on the bar and said goodbye to me in such a way that I knew he'd planned it in advance, hoping that I'd be looking in his direction.

I forgot all about him, I didn't expect him ever to come in again. But a week later he was back, and after that it was a regular thing. He came with his friends, and I really don't think it was because I was there; they were just a gang who met up regularly and were going through a phase of drinking in this particular pub. But he did remember me, and looked for me when he came in the door, and blushed if I served him. When his friends saw us chatting together they teased him. They made him go to the bar for every round, and then they whistled and laughed to encourage him.

—Go on, ask her, they said, meaning me to hear.

—Fuck off, he said, red-faced, pretending to be busy with the first mouthful of his pint.

Every time I saw him I'd feel the same shock at his likeness to Patrick. People come in physical types; I've seen girls I immediately recognised as belonging to the same type as me: small and round with these deep-lidded frog-eyes. There are dark ones and blonde ones, but the type is as unmistakable as if we belonged to the same subspecies. And, even though there were specific points on which they didn't match, this man and Patrick had the same overall effect. The man in the pub was blurred where Patrick was definite. His skin was coarser. His hair wasn't as black and straight: it was dark brown, with honey-brown curling bits in it. He was a little shorter than Patrick, but more muscular, as if he did physical work. I asked him, and he said he was a gas engineer, which wasn't all that physical, but presumably more strenuous than lecturing in literature of the Early Modern period. He had a little beer belly like Patrick's. His jeans hung on his narrow hips in the same way. Actually – oddly, considering how unlike their lives and personalities were – they even dressed the same. They wore tight V-necked sweaters over jeans, without a shirt. They wore black T-shirts with those little cap sleeves. I suppose they had both found the styles that suited them.

And soon something began that I'm shocked to think of now. Something that I initiated. It would never have occurred to him even to speak to me, beyond ordering his drinks, if I hadn't started it. I didn't just flirt with him. I went all out to make things go further. I knew this was a risky and demeaning strategy; it certainly wasn't something I'd ever done before. But with him I was safe because it didn't matter. It honestly wouldn't have mattered to me if he'd stopped coming to the pub and I'd never seen him again. So it could do no harm to play my game.

If I wasn't busy I'd watch him from my vantage point behind the bar. Sooner or later he'd become aware of this, and look up from where he stood or sat with his mates, and then I'd smile at him, a long heated-up smile, and he would redden and look away again, smiling too. When he came to the bar I rushed to serve him, even if one of the other staff was closer. He bought me drinks, and instead of thanking him and putting the money behind the bar as I usually did, I poured myself a Bacardi and Coke, clinked glasses with him, and asked him about himself. When I gave him his change I made sure our fingers touched. I don't think that anything like this had happened to him before. He wasn't a complete innocent. (I found out that he'd been engaged to someone and she had broken up with him a few months before.) But he wasn't used to being pursued by a stranger.

The shock of his looking so much like Patrick never completely left me. On the one hand, I felt I had the measure of the man he was, pleasant and rather dull. He and his friends talked all evening about cars and football, and teased each other in the explosive foot-shuffling, flaring-up way I remembered from the boys at school; from time to time they'd run out of things to say to one another and sit in silence, taking mouthfuls of their beer. On the other hand, his appearance flashed a promise to me, as if Patrick's qualities must be locked up inside him somewhere, if only I could find the key to release them.

Eventually I got him to the point where he couldn't help but ask me if he could give me a lift home after work. I felt embarrassed then, as if my game had gone too far. He waited for me while we cleared up, and reassured me that he'd only had one pint and was all right to drive, and then he led me proudly around the corner to his car, which looked very shiny under the street lamps. I hoped that he hadn't cleaned it for my benefit. I think he felt more confident about his car than about himself, but it was wasted on me, I couldn't tell one type of car from another. (Was it a Ford Focus? It might have been.) While he was driving me back to the house I shared with some other students, we both turned shy. I nervously asked him about his work, and he told me that he had worked for British Gas for several years and then set up his own business with a friend.

For reasons to do with the VAT they'd recently had to split the business into two, one side dealing with boilers and central-heating systems and the other with gas appliances, although in effect they still worked together. He explained this to me in some detail, and I was bored. I was hoping that none of my housemates would be around when I asked him in for coffee, and they weren't.

It was always better when he wasn't talking. I was glad that he didn't talk much. When he was silent I could recover the illusion I was in pursuit of. I hardly talked to him about myself – about college, about reading, about my plans. I hardly talked to him at all. I turned on my light, which had a pink bulb, so that the room was dim. I kissed him, I touched him, I undid his clothes, I made all the first moves. I don't think he was quite comfortable with the speed with which these things happened. He was a nice chap, he would have preferred to take things slowly. He would have preferred to have me as his proper girlfriend. On the other hand, he was a man; he didn't turn me down. Perhaps he felt a bit ashamed of himself afterwards. Or ashamed of me, more likely. I don't remember him staying long in my room, I don't remember watching him while he dressed to go home. I think he shared a flat with his brother and another man, but I never went there.

We didn't 'go out' together. We only ever did one thing together. For a couple of months, before I gave up my job at the pub and went home for the summer, we did that every week. Of course I was pretending the whole time that I was with Patrick, that it was Patrick who was making love to me. Only the pretence was never complete. Even in the dim light from the pink bulb, even if I half closed my eyes and didn't look directly at him, even when I was mixing up together in my mind the physical reality of our bodies grappling and one of my stories about Patrick, the knowledge that he wasn't Patrick seeped irresistibly in. This wasn't the real thing. It was only a second-hand enactment of love.

I have forgotten to give his name. His name was Dave.

It's only a few years ago but a lot has happened since then. Those are the years when a lot happens; when your life lurches across crucial transitions like a train hurtling across points at speed. It doesn't always feel like that at the time. At the time you sometimes feel that life has slowed down to a frozen stillness. There's no tedium like the tedium of twenty. But all the while you are in fact flying fast into a future decided by a couple of accidental encounters or scraps of dreams.

In the end, Patrick Hammett reached out for me. Unbelievably, what he actually said when he did it was something like he had always loved me, he had been fascinated by me from the moment I first walked into the lecture room. Or words to that effect. Which just goes to show how you mustn't trust a scrupulous realism, that sometimes sloppy fantasy comes nearer the true state of things. I became the person it had been unimaginable for me to be: Patrick's girlfriend, Patrick's wife. We had to wait until I wasn't his student any more before we could tell everyone about this, and those months were the most wonderful months, the secret months, when I had to sit in his classes and engage in discussion as usual, as if there was nothing going on between us.

I love Patrick. I think we're well matched. But of course I'm not infatuated with him any more, and it's a kind of relief when all that ends. You can't go on being infatuated with someone you share toothpaste with, whose crusty inside-out balls of socks you have to put into the washing machine. I haven't changed my mind about how intelligent and articulate he is; I count on that. But I'm irritated by the gulp of breath he takes before he pours out some hoarded-up information, and at how he works conversations around to an opportunity for him to be surprised at someone else's ignorance. When he's holding forth in an argument he fills any gaps while he searches for words with a loud 'um', so that no one else has a chance to break in with a different point of view.

I've never told Patrick about Dave. And I've never seen him since. I once looked up gas engineers in the Yellow Pages and found a company that might have been his; I couldn't look him up in the residential phone book because I never knew his surname. In my first few months with Patrick, if I ever thought about Dave I was just embarrassed at what I'd done. But then the idea of him began to preoccupy me, like an unsolved mystery. Why had he lent himself so unquestioningly, so pliably, to my fantasy? How did he explain to himself what was happening between us? I try to remember the details of our lovemaking and I can't. I can hardly believe that we were pressed naked against one another again and again. I feel as if I wasted something important, longing all the time for him to be someone else. What was he feeling, when he didn't speak?

There's no real equivalence, between my situation now and my situation then. I'm genuinely happily married to Patrick and given the chance would not even seriously consider throwing in my luck with a stranger I have nothing in common with. The little hunger of wasted opportunity only gets expressed in my fantasies, which contrive themselves in spite of me. No green lane, no gate into a wood. He's a gas engineer in the fantasy, of course. He comes to my house to mend the boiler. At first we pretend we don't recognise each other. I show him the problem and hover discreetly while he takes the front of the boiler off and crouches to look inside. He asks me to hand him a spanner from his toolbox; when he takes it from me he touches my hand with his.

I wish he wasn't a gas engineer. It sounds too much like a scenario from one of those funny sixties pornographic films, where the milkman or the postman is served up to the bored housewife amid all the conveniences of her own kitchen. But I've tried giving him other, outdoor, professions, and I didn't believe in them, they had no connection with the real man.

When he stands up to tell me there's a problem with the regulator, he steps towards me and begins to kiss me. It's then I see that what we did together has had consequences, for him. It has made him rather reckless, sexually. He has learned the audacity to reach across, through all the mess we make with thinking and talking, through to the body and the body's truth.

I have to be careful not to believe in this. It is only a dream.

EXCHANGES

Two friends are walking together round the new British Galleries at the Victoria and Albert Museum. These women look interesting. One is fine-boned, small, with crinkled black hair pinned up; she's wearing a green dress and a mohair cardigan. The other is taller and more awkward; her red hair is shoulder-length with a fringe. She has put gold-rimmed glasses on to look at the exhibits, but obviously doesn't like wearing them, because when they stop to talk she takes them off and dangles them dangerously on her finger. Once she drops them with a clatter but they are OK.

The new galleries are very hands-on; you can make a chair, design a coat of arms, identify porcelain. The women try on a crinoline over their clothes, they take turns to walk up and down in it.

—Oh, it's *nice*, see how it swings, it's very light.

—Wouldn't you just *clear space*?

—You could have a man inside, said one. —Imagine.

The women are at that age which on the outside is ambivalent: young and not-so-young are difficult to disentangle, in good clothes, in a good light, after a good life of the privileged kind of work that doesn't weather or wizen you. Inside, though, these years register for the women themselves, inexorably and determiningly as a clock ticking. There's a year when you're thinking anything could still happen, reproduction-wise (this either makes you hopeful or cautious, depending on what you want). Then there's a year when you think you never know (after all, Cherie Blair had one). And then there's a year when you think it isn't any way going to happen now, not without an improbable Old Testament miracle or the intervention of some crazed Italian doctor. These women are both, in fact, at this Old Testament stage, although they can both get away with looking as if they might not be.

One of them – Louie, the taller one with red hair – is a mother: she has two daughters. The dark one, Phil, is not. You can't tell this from looking at their bodies either, not from the outside: both are trim and slender. Perhaps you might guess, though, that Louie is the mother. Although she's more awkward than Phil, and probably thinks she's not as attractive, she's less self-conscious about parading up and down in the crinoline in front of other visitors. That might come from seeing herself reflected in the eyes of her daughters, who will love her or think her absurd however she tries, so that she doesn't need to try so hard. (In the early days of motherhood, she wouldn't have put it as positively as that: it felt sometimes as though she'd been taken out of her own possession and become no more than a rag doll for her daughters' entertainment. But now the girls are fifteen and twelve, and she's recovered, somewhat.)

In the museum café they talk unstoppably, as they always have done since they first got to know one another at college. They used to talk about men, with intensity and absorption: the rage against men was almost as stimulating as the sexual excitement men generated. Now all that's eased off. Sometimes Louie grumbles about Duncan, her husband, but the fervour's gone out of it. Once you've been together with someone for twenty years there's no excuse for hanging on with them if you think they're so awful: and of course she doesn't really think Duncan's awful, she supposes that she even loves him dearly, these days, underneath it all. Phil, on the other hand, has only been with Merrick for five years, and she's still tender about him and defensive, so that she won't reciprocate when Louie makes sniping remarks about his sex. Talking about men was more fun when Louie was really, really, planning on leaving Duncan, or at least having an affair with someone else; and when Phil was in the throes of a tormenting love for a no-good community activist who made her do things in bed that frightened her.

Now they talk about all kinds of other interesting subjects. Work, of course: Phil is a designer for a publisher, Louie works from home as a translator. And then about writing, painting, politics, parents. Phil's mother is very frail and may have to go into a home. Louie took her girls on the march against the war in Afghanistan. Both friends have, separately, seen the Auerbach exhibition: both were moved and disturbed by the monastic absolutism of his pursuit of truth. Louie confides in Phil (at tedious length, she fears) about the terrible struggle she is engaged in with her older daughter Ella, over Ella's attitude, over whether she's allowed out on her own in town, over what time she's supposed to come in if she is allowed out, and so on. Louie has noticed that when she begins to complain about Ella, Phil's expression tightens slightly: as if she is not completely, absolutely, on Louie's side.

When they have finished looking round the galleries Phil and Louie both go back to Phil's flat; they are hosting a meeting of their creative writing group there that evening, and Louie is staying over. Duncan is going to look after the girls (for once). Merrick is away (he is a rep for a wine company and often has to travel abroad).

Phil has been in this same small flat for years (from long before she knew Merrick): in the same period Duncan and Louie have moved three times, once with each promotion Duncan has had at the newspaper. Phil has a gift for making a place inviting: the shelves are piled with collections of books and objects, there are cushiony corners for reading. Everything promises retreat and solitude and concentration. Louie has never, in truth, liked any of her own houses as much as she likes it in here.

—I've brought you a present, says Louie. —I got this in the museum shop when you weren't looking.

Phil feels inside the paper bag: then she turns a strange face on her friend.

—Oh, Louie, she wails. —You've given me an egg.

Louie realises what she has done: she blushes darkly. The egg is an (expensive) replica of the kind that Victorian dairywomen put under hens to encourage them to lay: made in off-white porcelain with a grey crazing all over its surface. She had only wanted it because it was heavy and cold and smooth and she was bothered and footsore in the crowded shop.

—Don't you like it?

—Another egg! Phil laughs. —You really don't know you're doing it, do you? Merrick won't believe that you don't know; but I'm sure.

—I've never given you an egg before, have I?

Phil goes off into the front room and brings back a plate on which there is a whole collection of eggs: blown and painted ones, wooden ones, stone ones, one in burnished metal. The collection must have been out on display among all the other interesting things, on all the many evenings Louie has spent here.

—I gave you all those? When? Surely not. Some of them I've never seen before.

—All of them. Over the past — oh, five or six years?

—God: have you thought that I meant something by it? Some awful kind of hint?

—You tell me.

—No, honestly, Phil, if I really try to think, it's probably just that there's something contained and satisfying and . . . you know . . . elliptical . . . about the shape, which makes me think of you. Of how you are. That's all I can imagine.

—Only I'd rather, says Phil, —that we agreed that at this point my egg collection's complete. It's finished. There aren't ever going to be any chickens.

They only began writing about a year ago: but it has taken hold of them both with a ferocity and a destructive importance. Neither is satisfied with anything they've done, yet. There are five of them in the writing group: under its surface appearance of supportive and sane encouragement a kind of anarchy of need and self-doubt and competition runs loose. Phil and Louie agree privately that none of the other three are very good. Even more privately, they doubt one another. That evening Phil reads out a story about a love affair between an older woman and a boy: the paper shakes in her hands. Louie feels embarrassed for her: the story is unconvincing and mawkish. Because of the egg disaster, however, she feels absolutely unable to say anything critical about it; in fact she praises it exaggeratedly, singling out the one or two moments which could be read as if they were ironic.

—About these eggs, says Louie when the others have gone. —I feel so awful. But do you know what occurred to me? You're always giving me jugs.

—Jugs?

—Really. The Habitat one for my last birthday, that old blue and white spotted one, a big one with a leaf pattern you brought back from Portugal . . . Perhaps you mean something about me pouring myself out. Perhaps you mean that I'm wasting myself; giving myself away.

Phil sits with her feet tucked under her in a corner of the deep blue sofa. She doesn't seem very interested in the jugs. She tells Louie that what she wrote in the story, the older woman and the boy, really happened to her.

—You're joking, says Louie, slopping scalding tea. —You had a whole love affair, and never told me a word about it? When, for God's sake? Is this before Merrick?

Phil says that she finished it six months ago, that Merrick doesn't know. She says she finished it because it was really so unforgivable, he was the son of a friend of hers from work, someone Louie didn't know. He was eighteen.

—Not much older than Ella, says Louie.

—No.

—I don't know how you could.

—No.

But Phil sits with her face shining in some way – contained, oblique – which closes Louie out. She tells Louie that the boy was so special, so gifted, so lovely to look at. She tells her how they spent nights together at the seaside in Suffolk because his parents had a holiday place there, and how the room they slept in was full of his boyhood photographs and birdwatching lists and Airfix models. He was so completely serious about her. He was so concentrated. He had had no idea that things could be like that. (Louie supposes that 'things' means sex.) He had got a place to read English at Cambridge. (That was how it had all started: Phil's friend had asked her to give her son extra tuition for his English A level.)

—He met someone we both knew at a party the other day, Phil says. —He asked after me, and before they could say that I was fine, he filled up with tears. It was all right. The person just thought he had a crush.

—It's terrible, says Louie.

—I had to finish it because I didn't want to be with him and be fifty. Or anywhere near fifty.

Louie sits up late, alone, on the sofa that is now pulled out and made into a bed for her. She's beginning to remember all the writing Phil brought to the workshop while she must have been carrying on this ridiculous affair. How could she have failed to guess? How could she have thought those poems were about Merrick? The writing wasn't particularly good. Love makes you stupid, she thinks, that kind of love.

You couldn't be sorry that it wasn't going to happen to you, ever again.

She feels as if a door is closing painfully on her, squeezing her shut: she holds the cool porcelain laying-egg against her hot cheeks and her wrists. Was she burning with envy: would she, in truth, give anything to have what Phil had had, just one last time? She reviews the things she wouldn't give, not in her right mind: children, kindness, peace, writing. But then that kind of love has nothing to do with your right mind.

No, not 'never again'.

Surely not.

Not 'never', not yet, not quite.

A CARD TRICK

It was 1974: not a good year, clothes-wise, if you were an
eighteen-year-old girl, tall and overweight, with thick curling
hair and glasses. Gina liked best to wear a duffel coat, underneath which she imagined that she hid herself. But this was
summer, she was on holiday, and she had had reluctantly to
leave the duffel coat at home. She mostly wore a Laura Ashley
dress in blue sprigged cotton. It was meant to look as if it
had been faded by haymaking in meadows of wild flowers;
but its buttons gaped across her bust, it was tight around her
hips, and she knew its effect on her was not rustic but hulking
and penitentiary. Sometimes while she walked along bitter
tears stung her eyes, at the idea of the sheer affront of her
ugliness. At other times she was more hopeful.

Today at least the sun was not shining. When it shone –
and it had shone every day since she arrived – it made
things worse; it seemed such an insult to nature and beauty
not to want to peel off one's clothes and run around on
the beach, not to be happy. But today the sky was a soft
grey which kept dissolving into warm rain, and everybody
was more or less muffled under waterproofs. Because it was
raining, Mamie had driven inland with her from the house
on the coast, to visit Wing Lodge. Mamie was her mother's
friend, and Gina was staying with her and her family for a
fortnight; although to call her a friend did not quite explain
the whole thing, as Mamie was also a client, for whom her
mother made clothes.

Mamie told it as a great joke that she was an Honourable because her father had had some sort of title; Princess Margaret had once come to tea with her family. She was small and very pretty, with sloping shoulders and ash-blonde hair and a face that was always screwing up with laughter; her tan was the kind you can only get in the South of France (they had a house there too). Her clothes seemed effortless – today, for example, a Liberty print blouse under a cream linen pinafore – but Gina had seen some of these things in the making and knew how much effort actually went into them, the serious scrutiny of pinned-up hemlines in front of the mirror, the bringing things back ruefully, apologetically, after a week or two, with a nagging suspicion that a sleeve was set in too high, or an inspiration that the seams would look wonderful with two rows of over-stitching. She was being very kind – very encouraging – to Gina. She had not made any mention of the Laura Ashley dress, nor the hairslide that had seemed an appealing idea when Gina brushed her hair that morning but was now bobbing against her cheek, having slipped to a wrong and ridiculous place.

On their way to Wing Lodge they stopped off at a cottage café by the side of the country road; they were the only customers in a small room crowded with little toppling chairs and glass-topped wicker tables, smelling of damp and cake.

—It'll probably be instant coffee, whispered Mamie with conspiratorial amusement. (Gina only ever had instant at home.) —But I don't care: do you? Or we could risk the tea. And you've got to have a Danish pastry or something, to keep you going.

Mamie was probably making reference to the fact that Gina oughtn't to be eating pastries of any kind. Her diet, which alternated during this period of her life between punishing obedience and frantic transgression, had been thrown into such chaos since she'd been staying at Mamie's — on the one hand, she was too shy to refuse the things that were pressed upon her, on the other, she didn't dare to raid the fridge or the cupboards in between meals — that she didn't even know whether she was being good or not. She agreed to the pastry.

Gina had just had her A-level results — three As and two grade one S levels — and she was preparing for her Cambridge Entrance Examinations in November. Mamie professed an exaggerated awe of her cleverness.

—You really make me so ashamed, she said, when she had finished charming the elderly waitress and giving very exact instructions as to how she liked her tea ('pathetically weak, no milk, just pour it the very instant the water's on the leaves, I'm so sorry to be such a frightful nuisance'). —We're such duffers in my family. We've hardly got an O level between us: and that's after spending an absolute fortune on the children's education. Josh refused to go back to Bedales to do retakes. Becky left the day she was sixteen, she never even sat any exams. How I'd love for one of them to have your brains.

—I'm not that special, Gina lied, muffled through damp pastry flakes.

Somewhere in the deepest recesses of herself, Gina pitied Mamie and her children precisely along the lines Mamie suggested. The children — three older boys and a girl Gina's age — certainly weren't clever in the way she was. She'd never seen them reading a book, they hadn't known the other day at breakfast who Walter Gropius was, she was sure they were sublimely ignorant about all the things that seemed to her to matter most: literature and painting and the history of ideas. But Becky and Josh and Tom and Gabriel had every advantage on the surface in the here and now, in envy of which Gina was horribly ready to abase herself. Mamie was surely disingenuous in praising up her brains. She was just being kind, she wouldn't have exchanged brains, really, for the easy personable charm that all her children had, not if brains meant awkward bodies and thick glasses.

Mamie's children might not be clever, but they didn't actually say stupid things, as Gina did, tongue-tied with bookish awkwardness. On the contrary, they were funny and chatty and informed about practical matters. They were indifferent to politics, but sincerely charming and generous with the lady who came to clean and cook and iron for them every day, whereas Gina didn't know how to talk to her. They were masters of arts that Gina knew she could never be competent in, however hard she tried: tennis, for example, and motorbiking, and snorkling. She couldn't even ride a pushbike. They had tried to persuade her to put on a wetsuit to swim in; her resistance must have seemed fanatical. All the boys could sail, and had the use of their father's boat; Gabriel and Josh were preparing to take it to the Bahamas in September.

Gabriel, the oldest, had a darkroom and developed his own photographs. Becky posed for him unembarrassed, arranging her face to look its best. If ever Gabriel turned the camera on Gina she swivelled away, protesting and sulking; so he soon stopped trying. The house was filled with vivid laughing photographs in which the lives of this family seemed poignant and enchanting even beyond anything you could grasp in everyday contact with them. Gina studied the photographs with the same yearning she felt looking at fashion pictures in magazines: trying to learn how one might possess oneself with such certainty, know so confidently how to live.

They were all beautiful. Gabriel and Becky looked like Mamie, small with pretty puppy-dog faces, turned-up noses and huge eyes. The others looked like their father, who was in France with friends. (This separation seemed strange to

Gina, whose parents did everything together: her mother had hinted, out of confidences given her when she was crawling round a hemline with her mouth full of pins, that all was not well in Mamie's marriage. Dickie's absence was a relief, anyway. Gina had seen him once or twice when he came to pick up Mamie after a fitting: tanned with white teeth, savagely impatient.) Tom and Josh – Josh was the nearest boy to Gina in age – were tall, with slim brown bodies, fine skin taut over light strong bones, long sensitive-knuckled hands and feet. She got used to their near-naked-ness on the beach, in swimming trunks, or bare-chested in cut-off jeans. It was 1974: they wore their sun-bleached hair long and they walked barefoot everywhere.

The spare bedroom Gina stayed in was on the ground floor and opened on to the hall, whose dark parquet was always dusted with a layer of fine sand blown in from the beach. Sometimes when she peeped out of her door to see if the coast was clear to visit the bathroom (she was 'working', she told them, at the little table Mamie had set up for her), she saw prints of the boys' bare feet in the sand, crossing the hall to the kitchen or to the stairs. For some reason this moved her, and her heart clenched in an excitement more breathlessly sexual than if she'd actually seen the boys themselves.

The visit to Wing Lodge had been part of the pretext for Gina coming to visit Mamie in the first place. It was the house where her favourite novelist had lived, and she had wanted to make a pilgrimage there; but she was beginning to wish that she could have come on her own. She was burdened by her sense of Mamie's kindness: Mamie had clearly never read any of Morrison's books, so she could have no good reason, surely, to want to see his house. Gina worried over the things that Mamie would probably rather have done, and in more congenial company. They arrived in the little town and found Wing Lodge in one of the oldest streets, behind the church, in a walled front garden which even in the rain was lovely: pale roses bowed and dripping with water, a crumbling sundial, a path of old paving stones set into the grass, wandering to a bench under a gnarled apple tree.

—Isn't it just charming? Mamie exclaimed, pausing in the porch to shake off the umbrella which she had gallantly insisted in sharing with Gina, so that they were now both wet. —This is such a treat. Thank you so much for bringing me here. I can't imagine why I've never been before.

Gina had thought that at last, at Wing Lodge, she would be on home ground. She knew so much about this writer: a friend of Conrad and Ford, given a complimentary mention by Henry James in 'The New Novelists'. She had written the long essay for her English A level on his use of complex time schemes. She loved the spare texture of his difficult sad books, and felt that she was exceptionally equipped to understand them. Faced with his most obscure passages (he wasn't elaborate like James but compressed and allusive) she trusted herself to intuit his right meaning, even if she couldn't quite disentangle it yet, syntactically. But as she followed Mamie through the front door into the low-ceilinged hall, she realised that she was not entering one of Morrison's books, where she could feel confident; she was entering his house, where she might not. Two middle-aged ladies presided at a table over leaflets and a cash box and tickets; wood panelling polished to a glow as deep and savoury as conkers reflected the yellow light from a couple of lamps; tall vases of flowers stood against the wall on the uneven stone-flagged floor. Gina stepped flinchingly around a Persian rug that opened like a well of colour under her feet.

—This is Gina, Mamie said to the ladies while she got out her purse to pay. —She's the daughter of a very gifted and creative friend of mine. We're here today because she loves this writer's books so much and has written her A-level essay about him. She's very, very bright, and is taking her Cambridge Entrance in the autumn.

Their smiles at Gina were coldly unenthusiastic. They advised the visitors to start in the room on the right and make their way around to the study, which was arranged as it had been in the writer's lifetime. If they went upstairs at the end of the tour they would find an exhibition of editions of the works. —Which might interest you, one of them suggested sceptically.

The house was furnished — sparely, exquisitely — with a mixture of antiques and curiosities and modern things: a venerably worn Indian tapestry thrown across an old chaise longue, an elm art deco rocking chair, drawings by Wyndham Lewis and Gaudier-Brzeska. It was dark everywhere and the lamps were switched on in the middle of the day: the low, deeply recessed casement windows were running with rain and plastered with wet leaves. Mamie moved through the rooms in a kind of hushed rapture.

—So sweet! she whispered emphatically. —What a darling place. What treasures.

Gina thought perplexedly of the letters Morrison had written from Wing Lodge: full of damp walls and leaking roofs and smoking chimneys and penetrating cold, as well as self-deprecating confessions of untidiness and neglect. The writer had never made much money: she hadn't imagined that his house would be like this. How could he have afforded these kind of possessions? The rooms were like Mamie's rooms: glossy with value and distinction, a kind of patina of initiated good taste.

—Do they live here? she asked. —Those ladies.

—Oh, I should think so, wouldn't you? It feels very much a home rather than a musem. The widow stayed on here, apparently, until she died a few years ago. So I suppose they've just kept a few of the rooms as she left them. It's only open a couple of afternoons a week.

There was a photograph of Anne, the American wife and widow, on the plain writing table in the study: young, with a Katherine Mansfield fringe and bobbed hair and a necklace of beads the size of cherries. Morrison had been a world-wanderer, with a Scottish father and a Norwegian mother (you could feel the influence of a certain Scandinavian neurasthenia in his novels). He had settled down at last to marriage here in the south of England, and written his best books here, and died here, in his fifties, in 1942.

—Can't you just imagine being able to write, at this desk? said Mamie encouragingly.

Gina looked at her dumbly across the charming room with its waxed floor slanting quaintly to the window, its framed woodcuts on the walls. It seemed unlikely to her that anyone could ever write anything worth reading in a place like this. She thought of art as a concealed ferocity; writers were like the Spartan boy carrying the fox under his shirt. What could one do, set up in the too-complete loveliness of this room: write cookery books perhaps, or a nostalgic memoir? At the same time she was filled with doubt, in case she was deluded, in case it turned out after all that art and the understanding of art was a closed club she would never be able to enter, she who had never owned one thing as beautiful as the least object here.

Sometimes Gina came out victorious from her struggle with Mamie's pressing hospitalities, and succeeded in staying at home when everyone else went to the beach. (The sea was only a few minutes' walk from the front door across the dunes, but the beach they liked best for swimming and surfing was a short drive away.) She heard and winced at the little crack of impatience in Mamie's voice – 'I suppose it's awfully good of you, to want to have your head buried in a book all day' – but that was worth incurring, in exchange for the freedom of having the house to herself for hours on end.

She didn't really spend all that time studying. She drifted from her books to the windows to the cupboards in the kitchen, eating whatever Mamie had left for her almost at once, and then spooning things out of expensive jars from the delicatessen (only enough so that no one could ever tell) and ferreting out the forgotten ends of packets of cakes and biscuits and nuts. She made herself comfortable with her bare legs up over the back of the collapsed chintz sofa, hanging her head down to the floor to read Becky's copies of *Honey* and *19*. She took possession of the lovely weather-washed old house with a lordly offhandedness she never felt when the others were around. She ran herself copious baths perfumed with borrowed Badedas in the old claw-foot tub with its thundering taps. She tried on Mamie's lipstick and Becky's clothes. She browsed through the boys' bedrooms with their drawn curtains and heaps of salty sandy beach gear and frowsty sock-smells; she experimented with their cigarettes and once for an hour lost herself over a magazine of dizzyingly explicit sexual photographs she found stuffed down between one bed and the wall (she didn't know whose bed it was, and the next time she felt for the magazine it had gone). She sat in a deckchair on the sagging picturesque veranda whose wood was rain-washed to a silvered grey, drinking Campari in a cocktail glass with a cherry from a bottle and a dusty paper umbrella she found in a drawer: afterwards she cleaned her teeth frantically and chewed what she hoped were herbs from the garden, so no one would smell alcohol on her breath.

Once, after about an hour of this kind of desultory occu-pation of the place, she happened to glance up through the open French windows from her dangling position on the sofa and was stricken with horror: she had been sure they had all gone to the beach (except Gabriel, who was back in London), but there was Tom, stripped to the waist, cutting the meadow of long grass behind the house with a scythe, working absorbedly and steadily with his back to her. Tom was particularly frightening: moody like his father, dissenting and difficult enough even to have required at some point consultations with psychologists (this from more confidences over the pins and pattern-cutting). Actually, he was the one Gina chose most often for her fantasies, precisely because he was difficult: she imagined herself distracting, astonishing, taming him.

Appalled to think what he might have seen of her in her rake's progress around his mother's house, she scuttled to her bedroom, where she spent the rest of the long day in a state of siege, not knowing whether he knew she was there or not, paralysed with self-consciousness, avoiding crossing in front of her own bedroom window, unable to bring herself to venture out from her room even when she was starving or desperate to pee. Tom came inside – perhaps for lunch or perhaps because he'd finished scything – and played his Derek and the Dominoes album loudly as though he believed he had the house to himself. Gina lay curled in a foetal position on the bed. She dreaded that he might open the door and find her, but dreaded too that if he didn't find her, and then learned that they had shared the house for the whole afternoon without her even once appearing, he would think her – whom he mostly scarcely noticed – something grotesque, insane, something that deserved to live under a stone.

She wept silently into her pillow, wishing he'd go, and even at the same time mourning this opportunity slipping away, this long afternoon alone in the house together that was after all the very stuff of her tireless invention. They might have conversed intelligently over coffee on the veranda; she might have accepted one of his cigarettes and smoked it with offhanded sophistication; surprised at her thoughtfulness and quiet insight, he might have held his hand out to her on impulse to take her walking with him down among the dunes. And so on, and so on, down to the crashing inevitable too-much-imagined end.

When Gina was at her unhappiest during that fortnight, she wanted to blame her mother. Her mother had been so keen on her taking up Mamie's invitation: ostensibly because she worried that Gina was studying too hard, but really because of a hope, which had never been put into words but which Gina was perfectly well aware of, that Gina might get on with Mamie's boys. 'Get on with': it wouldn't have been, not for her mother, any more focused than that; a vague idea of friendly comradeship, the boys coming through daily unbuttoned summertime contact to appreciate Gina's 'character', as her mother optimistically conceived of it. Boys, her mother obviously thought, would be good for Gina; they might help to make her happy. But her mother wasn't solely responsible. When the holiday was suggested, Gina had had to be coaxed, but she hadn't refused. She must have held out hopes too: less innocent hopes, grotesquely and characteristically misplaced.

There came another day of rain. At the end of a long afternoon of Monopoly and a fry-up supper Mamie was desperate, shut up with her charm and a crowd of disconsolate young ones in the after-aroma of sausages and chips. When she proposed a surprise visit to friends who had a place twenty miles along the coast, she hardly bothered to press Gina to join them, or Josh, either, who was building card houses on the table and said he didn't want to go. She and Becky and Tom set off with bottles of wine and bunches of dripping flowers from the garden; the sound of escape was in their voices calling back instructions and cautions, Tom shaking the car keys out of his mother's laughing reach, saying she couldn't manage his old car, which needed double declutching.

Gina was going home the next day. Mamie would run her into town to catch the train. Probably that was the explanation for the comfortable flatness she felt now: it didn't even occur to her to mind either way that Josh had stayed. She knew with a lack of fuss that it had nothing to do with her: he had stayed because he didn't feel sociable and because he was idly fixated on a difficulty he was having with the card houses. The sound of the car driving off sank down and dissolved into the rustle of the rain, behind which, if she pushed her hair back behind her ears to listen, she could hear the waves of the sea, undoing and repairing the gravel on the beach. When Gina had finished putting away the dishes she sat down opposite Josh, watching him prop cards together with concentrating fingers; she was careful not to knock the table or even to breathe too hard. They talked, speculating seriously about why it was that he couldn't make a tower with a six-point base; he had built one right up to its peak from a three and a four and a five base, but he had been trying and failing for hours to do a six. Josh had a loose, full lower lip which made his grin shy and qualified. There was silky fair beard growth on his chin and upper lip. He was gentler than his brothers, and had a slight lisp.

There was a second pack of cards on the table, rejected for building towers because the corners were too soft: Gina picked it up and fiddled with it on her lap without Josh noticing. The six-base tower came down in a shout of frustration, and Josh washed his hands groaning in the mess of cards.

—D'you want me to show you a card trick? Gina asked.

—OK, he said. —Anything. Just don't let me begin another one of these.

—Actually, I'm not going to do it, she said, —you are.

Put those cards out of the way. We'll use this older pack. It feels more sympathetic.

He was amiable, obliging, clearing the table, his eyes on her now to see what she could do.

—I'm going to give you power, she said. —I'm going to make you able to feel what the cards are, without looking at them. You're going to sort them into red and black. It's not even something I can do myself. Look.

She pretended to guess, frowning and hesitating, dealing the top few cards face down into two piles. —I don't know. Black, red; black, black, black; red, red. Something like that. Only I don't have this magic. I'll turn them over. See? All wrong. But you're going to have this power. I'm going to give it to you. Give me your hands.

He put his two long brown hands out palm down on the table; she covered them with her own and closed her eyes, squeezing slightly against his bony knuckles, feeling under the ball of her thumb a hangnail loose against the cuticle of his. Really, something seemed to transfer between them.

—There, she said briskly. —Now you've got the power. Now you're going to sort out these cards into black and red, face down, without looking. Black in this pile, red in this. Take your time. Try to truly feel it. Concentrate.

Obediently he began to deal the cards into two piles, doing it with hesitating wincing puzzlement, like someone led blindfold and expecting obstacles, laughing doubtingly and checking with her. —I have no idea what I'm doing here.

—No, you have. You really have. Trust it.

He gained confidence, shrugged, went faster: black, red, black, black, red, black, red, red, red . . . Halfway through she asked him to change round: red cards on the right, now, and black cards on the left pile. —Readjust: don't lose it. It's really just to keep you concentrating.

Then when he'd put down his last card and looked at her expectantly, she swept up the two piles and turned one over in front of his eyes. —So you see, if it's worked, this one should run from red to black . . . Look, there you are!

She spread the second pile, reversing it so that it seemed to run the other way. —And this one here, from black to red . . .

—Oh, no. No! That's just too weird. That's really weird, man. How did you *do* that? Jesus! He laughed in delighted bafflement, looking from the cards up to her face and back again.

She was laughing too, hugging her secret. —Do you want me to do it again, see if you can guess? Only hang on a sec, I need the loo . . .

He never guessed, he didn't notice that she took the second pack of cards with her to the bathroom to make them ready. ('Shall we use these newer ones, see if it works with them?') Gina couldn't quite believe that he couldn't see what she was doing. She had worked it out for herself, the first time that the trick was done on her.

—It's just spooky, he said in awe, shaking his head. —It doesn't make sense. There's just no way I should be getting these right. You must be *making* me deal them right, somehow . . .

—No, it's you, it's you, she insisted. —I can't do it. It's only you.

He wouldn't let her tell him how it was done, although she was longing to explain. He was right: it was better to hold off the climactic revelation with its aftermath of grey; the power of the mystery he couldn't break was a warm pleasure, satisfying and sensual between them. They ran their eyes over each other's faces in intimate connection, smiling; he brimmed with puzzlement and she was replete with knowledge. Then the moment slipped away; they gave up the trick after the third time, and played Mastermind and battleships, and exchanged talk in low, lax friendly voices. The others returned, crashing down through the garden, tipsily exalted. When Gina climbed between the sheets in her pyjamas, she found a warm pleasure persisting, a soft surprising parcel under her lungs; she examined it, and thought that it was probably happiness, a small preparatory portion of the great ecstasies she supposed life must have in store for her.

It was twenty-five years before she visited Wing Lodge again.

This time she was alone. She remembered that she had been there before, with Mamie, although she couldn't quite imagine why she had been staying with her: there had never been any real intimacy between their families. Dickie and Mamie had divorced not long after that holiday, and Mamie had died recently. One of the boys had drowned, years ago, she couldn't remember which one (she would have to ask her mother). The visit, now, was uncharacteristic of Gina. She never went to stately homes or birthplaces, and she deplored the heritage industry; she gave ironic lectures at her university on the enthusiasm of the masses for traipsing humbly and dotingly round the houses where they would once, and only sixty years ago, have been exploited as estate hands or scullery maids. But then this was an unsettled time in her life, and she was doing uncharacteristic things. She was making her mind up whether to embark on a full-scale new relationship; she had been divorced five years earlier, and now her lover wanted to move in. On impulse, leaving her son with friends for the weekend, she had booked herself into a hotel and come down to this little town to be alone, to think.

She hadn't imagined that she would actually go inside Wing Lodge, although she had been aware, of course, that the town she had chosen to think in was the one where

John Morrison, who was still her passion, had spent his last years. She had perhaps had a quixotic idea that by moving around in his streets she might arrive at his clarity; needless to say the streets remained just streets, full of cars and tourists; and for someone used to London, there weren't many of them to explore. With determined austerity, she had not brought any books away with her, imagining this would concentrate her mind. But the habit of years was too strong to break; over drawn-out coffees in the wood-panelled tea room, where the waitresses really did still wear white frilled aprons, she found herself reading the menu over and over, and then the ancient injunction against asking for credit in red calligraphy above the till, and then the left-behind sports pages of a newspaper. In the end she joined the little party of visitors being taken round Wing Lodge because there wasn't anything else to do. She was a middle-aged woman now, tall and statuesque in a tan linen Max Mara skirt and jacket; in her mass of thick dark curls grey hairs were sprouting with a coarse energy which made her suspect that age was going to impose itself differently to how she had imagined: less entropy, more vigorous takeover. However she tried to shrink it to size, her habit of authority was conspicuous. There were copies of her book about the novels in the little bookshop upstairs, but she wasn't going to own up to that; she followed the guide obediently about and listened with amusement to the way the wonderful works abounding in disruptive energy became, in the retelling, so much sad sawdust, so much lament, as Pound had put it, for the old lavender.

She wondered sceptically, too, whether the place was really arranged as Morrison would have known it. He and his wife had never had much money, even in the years of his critical success, and the couple were famous for their indifference to creature comforts. Friends complained that although the conversation was excellent you never got a

decent meal or a good night's sleep at Wing. Gina recognised one or two drawings she knew Morrison had
possessed, and a few things he might have brought back
from the East; but it must have been his wife who made
Wing Lodge into this tasteful cosy little nest, after he died,
when she inherited money from her family in America.
No doubt the frail ladylike guide and her possibly lesbian
frail ladylike companion, who must live here quietly
together on the days when they were not intruded upon
by a curious public, had added their bit of polish to the
deep old charm.

In the study, where Morrison's writing table was set out
with pens and notebooks, as if he had just this minute
stepped out for a walk in the fields in search of inspiration, there was also a shallow locked glass case in which
were displayed first editions of the novels and some of his
longhand drafts, as well as the copies that Anne had typed
up on her Olivetti, scribbled furiously over in his dark soft
pencil. Gina had handled his notebooks and typed manu-
scripts, and was familiar with his processes of composition.
When the others had moved on, she peered closely into
the case at one of the notebooks. These longhand drafts
were not difficult to read, although his handwriting was
odd, with large capitals and crunched-up lower case. She
recognised the text immediately. It was the scene in *Winter's
Day* when the middle-aged daughter declares her love for
the doctor, in the house where her father is dying. They
have left him with the nurse for an hour, and the doctor
is trying to persuade Edith to take some rest. A lamp is
burning although there is daylight outside the windows;
they are surrounded by the overspill of chaos from the sick-
room, basins and medicines and laundry. Edith tells the
doctor, who is married, that what she can't bear is that
when her father is dead he won't be coming to visit any
more. 'Because we shan't have our talks – you could have

no idea, because you're a man and you have work to do, of what these mean to me. My life has been so stupidly empty.' She presses her face, wet with tears, against the wool sleeve of his jacket. The doctor is shocked and offended, that Edith's mind is not on her father. Also, he is not attracted to her: he thinks with pity how plain she looks, haggard from exhaustion, and with bad teeth.

There weren't many corrections to this passage in the notebook. It was a kind of climax, an eruption of drama in a novel whose texture was mostly very quiet. But Morrison must have cut the scene in a later draft; in the published book all Edith said when she broke out was: 'Because we shan't have our talks . . . I will miss them.' Gina's eyes swam with tears as she bent over the case, reading the words. She was astonished: she never cried, she never got colds, so she didn't even have a tissue in her bag. Luckily, she was alone: she wiped her face on the back of her hand, and decided not to follow the rest of the party upstairs to the bookshop. Instead she made her way out into the exquisitely blooming back garden, and found a seat in a bower overgrown with Nelly Moser clematis and some tiny white roses with a sweet perfume.

Why did it move her, this scene of the woman giving away power over herself? It ought to disgust her, or fill her with rage – or relief, that a whole repertoire of gestures of female abasement was at last, after so many centuries, culturally obsolete. No one would dream of using a scene like that in a novel now. That wet face, though, against the rough wool sleeve, sent Gina slipping, careering down the path of imaginary self-abandonment. (Was the sleeve still there in the published version? She couldn't for the moment remember for sure.) She could almost smell the wool and imagine its hairy taste against her mouth, although none of the men she had loved ever wore that kind of tweedy jacket, except her father, perhaps, when she was a little girl.

It was sexual, of course, and masochistic: female exposed nakedness rubbing up against coarse male fibre; the threat of abrasion, of an irritated reaction on the finer, more sensitised, wet female surface.

You could see how it all worked. You could rationally resist it, and you could even – and here was the answer, perhaps, to the question that had brought her down to Wing Lodge in the first place – feel sure that you would never be able to surrender yourself like that, ever again. And yet the passage had moved her to unexpected tears. There was something formally beautiful and powerful and satisfying in it: that scene of a woman putting her happiness into a man's hands. Beside it, all the other, better, kinds of power that women had nowadays seemed, just for one floundering moment, second best.

Gina sat for a long time. A bee, or some bee-like insect, fell out of the flowers on to her skirt, and she was aware of the lady guide looking at her agitatedly from the French windows, probably wanting to close up the house. There came to her, in a flood of regret for her youth, the memory of a card trick, the one where you sorted the pack into black and red in advance, so that your victim wouldn't be able to put a card down wrong.

THE EGGY STONE

We found the Eggy Stone that first afternoon of the school camp.

As soon as we had dumped our things in the big khaki canvas tents, each with eight metal bedsteads in two rows, the teacher took us down to the sea. We crunched in socks and sandals across a rim of crisped black seaweed and bone and sea-washed plastic: the tide was in, the long grey line of the waves curled and sucked at the cramped remainder of the beach, a narrow strip of pebbles. For the moment we weren't allowed to go near the water. Under our sandals the big pale pebbles rattled and shifted awkwardly. The boys began throwing them in the sea; we felt between them for treasures, the creamy spirals from old shells, bits of washed-soft glass.

Her hand and mine found the Eggy Stone at the same moment, our fingers touched, and somehow that sealed it: I was hers and she was mine for the duration of the holiday. We had never been friends before. I didn't deserve her; she had only been in the school for a few months, but her status was clear, she had been put to sit the very first day on the table where the charming girls sat. I was clever: but she was blonde and daintily neat, with that fine pink skin the light almost seems to shine through. She had a pencil case full of the right kind of felts and danced with the other favoured girls in the country-dancing team that did 'Puppet on a String' instead of 'Trip to the Cottage'.

Even her name was pretty: Madeleine. I was ready to adore her.

She was fragile but firm. It was she who named the stone and held it out on her palm for me to share. It was small and egg-shaped and dull black, with a ring of white crystal teeth around it at one end, just where you would cut the top off an egg to eat it. If it hadn't become, the moment we chose it, 'the Eggy Stone', it would have been nothing special: there were hundreds and thousands more pebbles just as interesting. Madeleine began the cult, but I elaborated it. We took it in turns to hold the Eggy Stone, and the turns were decided by various ritualised competitions, including folded-paper fortune tellers, knocking the heads off plantains, and a kind of wrestling we invented, kneeling opposite each other with the stone placed between us and swaying in each other's arms, trying to force our opponent to touch ground on one side or another. Before each competition there was a form of words: something like 'Eggy Stone / On your own / All alone / Inaccessible light'. I was probably the one who made it up (although it owed something to a hymn we sang at school). I had a bit of a reputation as a poet; whereas Madeleine was the kind of girl who chanted things by rote and knew all the skipping rhymes and all the variations for games like 'Please Jack may we cross the water?'

Whoever possessed the stone felt privileged and secure for as long as it lasted. The sensation of it, smooth and warmed and resistant in the hand, came to be an end in itself, a real pleasure; and whoever didn't possess it yearned for it, until the moment arrived for another challenge. Once or twice Madeleine cheated, pushing her hand into my pocket and filching the stone without any contest, showing me with her quick brilliant smile that any appearance of fair play was only ever granted by her favour. I was outraged and helpless then, thrown back upon a self no longer complete without her. But mostly the passing of the stone was kind between us, an extraordinary bond. We went about with arms draped round one another's necks, and all Madeleine's usual friends included me tolerantly in their circle. We took it in turns to hold the stone at night, in the dark, in our sleeping bags (we slept in different tents).

The cult of the Eggy Stone didn't seem any stranger than all the other strangenesses, in a week away from home. Misery and wonder were flooded together: gargantuan preparations in the kitchen where we took our turn at helping cater for the children from seven schools; Madeleine and I trailing hand in hand, ankle-deep in tepid sea-foam; cocoa made with water and served in tin mugs; dread of the publicity of the toilets and consequent constipation. Some of the girls (Madeleine, but not me) crept out at night to kiss the boys in their tents. We learned new obscenities: 'min' and 'omo' among them (or at least that's how I heard them), which mystifyingly were also the names of cleaning products. On the last night the teachers made a campfire and taught us songs with accompanying actions. *Indians are high-minded, / Bless my soul they're double-jointed, / They climb hills and don't mind it, / All day long.* Madeleine beside me touched toes and reached her arms in the air with a pretty equanimity, as if whatever she was doing at a given moment was the only graceful thing possible.

I asked her the next morning, on the beach, before we got on the coach to go home, what we were going to do with the Eggy Stone. She took the stone from her pocket, holding it out reflectively on her hand for a moment; her pretty face was quite clear of either malice or tenderness. I had a proposal ready, that we should keep the thing for a week each, changing over every Monday, dividing up the holidays. I was not foolish enough to imagine that the magical game was going to carry on between us, once school camp was over. But before I could speak, Madeleine

turned and threw the Eggy Stone, hard and far, with a
confidence that made it clear she would one day be captain
of the netball team. I heard it land with a rattle among all
the other pebbles and knew that even if I went to look I
would never, ever be able to find exactly the same stone
again.

MATRILINEAL

One night forty years ago Helen Cerruti left her husband. They were living together at the time with their two little girls on the top floor of a big Edwardian house, in a respectable street where the houses sat back behind well-tended gardens, and pollarded lime trees with blotchy bark surged up like life forces out of the civilised pavement. The Cerruti girls taking in the terrain at pushchair level saw how dogs left their small calcinous offerings among the tree roots (the dogs in those days were fed only on bones and scraps). This was just at the end of the time when women walked and pushed pushchairs in those streets in gloves, with matching handbags and shoes, suffused in that vanished elegance at once studied and nonchalant.

Helen and Phil Cerruti didn't have much money – Phil was a jazz musician, who also gave lessons at the teacher-training college – but Helen had a gift for making herself elegant. She passed all her wisdom on to her girls, who later, in a different world, weren't really ever able to make much use of it: that it was better to have two or three good things in your wardrobe than to have it stuffed full with inferior items; that cut and line were important above all; that instead of washing your clothes to rags you should valet them carefully, taking out stains with patent cleaner from a bottle, repairing with a needle and thread, pressing everything through a wet cloth before you wore it. They had an intimation – seeing their mother in her petticoat pressing and steaming, pinning up and letting down and taking in, grimacing at her make-up in the mirror, practising postures – of the hidden heavy labour that underlay the nonchalant surface. Helen was a dancer; that is, she had been a dancer before she had her children. She still had a dancer's figure, driftwood washed to leanness. In 1965 she was wearing shirt dresses and pale pink lipstick; her dark hair was cut short, backcombed up behind a broad hairband.

The access to their top-floor flat was up a metal staircase added on to the side of the house, which gave out a booming noise however quietly you tried to step. If the Cerrutis had too many visitors, or Phil ran back two at a time because he'd forgotten something, or Nia rapt in one of her daydreams came stomping up, a heavy stolid little thing, after playing out in the garden, then the retired Reverend Underwood who lived with his wife on the floor below would pull back the net curtains and rap on the windows at them. Helen made Phil climb up in his socks when he came in after playing late at night, with his shoes in his hand, unless it was raining. She also feared that if he'd been drinking he'd slip on those damn stairs and break his neck. And the stairs meant she had to keep Sophie's pushchair down in the garage where Phil kept the car. Every expedition, even round the corner to the grocer's, or to the clinic for Sophie's orange juice, was a performance; when they got home she had to climb the stairs with Sophie struggling in her arms, laden with her shopping bags, clinging on to the metal handrail, desperate not to look down. Nia would go first and be entrusted with the keys. Straining on her stout legs she could just reach the keyhole. Solemn with her own importance, each time not quite believing that the trick would work, she would stagger forwards, hanging on to the keys, as the door swung in upon the familiar safe scene, extraordinarily unchanged since the moment they'd gone out, which would by now seem to Nia like hours and long ages ago.

Helen left Phil on an April evening, at about half past six. They had parted at breakfast on perfectly friendly terms; then one of Phil's lessons had been cancelled in the afternoon, which meant less money, and she had heard him bounding up the stairs, pleased of course at the release, a couple of hours before she expected him. She wasn't ready for him; she'd taken advantage of Sophie's afternoon nap to wash the linoleum in the kitchen, and was on her hands and knees in her oldest slacks, with her hair tied up in a scarf. Nia was leading one of her dolls on an adventure round the lounge, instructing it confidingly: along the bookcases made of planks and bricks, behind the jazz records, among the hilly cushions on the low couch covered in olive green, through the forest of the goatskin rug whose skin peeled in scraps that looked like tissue paper. The weather was grey, the clouds had been suffused all day with a bright light that never quite broke through them. Helen had all the windows open up here in the flat, she hated stuffiness; they were so high at the top of the house that they looked out into the hearts of the garden trees almost as if they were birds nesting. It was that suspenseful moment in spring when the cold has loosened its grip, the tender leaves are bursting out everywhere, a bitter green smell tugs at the senses. The adults are all poised for something momentous to happen to fill out the meaning of this transformation, anxious already in case another year is slipping past without certainty, without anything becoming clear.

—That's a very attractive proposition, said Phil when he came in and saw her scrubbing the floor intently with her back to him, her bottom stuck up in the air. He ran his hand suggestively around the curve of it under the tight cloth.

She looked over her shoulder at him, resting her weight

on one arm, wiping her sweaty face on her shirtsleeve. —
You're early.

—Cancellation, he said jubilantly. —Freedom! I've come
home to practise.

Usually, when she was ready for him, Helen made an
effort to be welcoming when Phil came home: to have a
meal ready, to freshen up her make-up and perfume, to take
an interest in whatever he'd been doing. She had herself
had a perfectly nice day. She had taken the girls to the park
on the way back from the shops this morning; this evening
when Phil went to play she was going to cut out the new
chunky white cotton drill she had bought to make a suit
to wear to his sister's wedding. She didn't even mind washing
the floor. She was sorry for Phil, having to go out and teach
when he hated it.

—But you can't practise here, she said.

This was their oldest quarrel, ever since they'd moved
from their first flat to this one, after Nia was born.

—They won't be in, he said easily, as if they hadn't been
over all this so many times before. —They won't mind.

—Why didn't you stay and practise at the college?

—Because I hate the college. Because I can't wait to
shake the stinking dust of the college off my shoes.

—But at college they have soundproof rooms.

He stood quietly then for a few moments without
moving; Helen pretended not to notice his portentousness,
swirling the scrubbing brush in her bucket of water.

—Do you really hate my music so much, Phil said: not
as a question but in a sort of wondering cold calm.

Phil Cerruti was a very good alto player, something in
the style of Art Pepper but of course not that good. Art
Pepper was his hero; he played his records over and over,
he learned his solos off by heart. He got a lot of work, in
the city in the west of England where they lived and the
area round about, but not enough work yet to give up

teaching. Helen loved him to play. She had fallen in love with him watching him onstage: his small loose-jointed body, its movements delicate and finished as a cat's, twitching to the off-beat. Moods passed visibly, like weather, over the transparent white skin of his face, blue under his eyes when he was tired. Men were drawn to Phil as well as women; his energy was a steady heat, a promise. He walked out of the kitchen without another word and went into the lounge. Helen went on scrubbing the floor for a while and then she got to her feet with her scrubbing brush still in her hand, and followed after him as if she had something more to say. Phil was sitting on the couch beside the open alto case, wetting the reed in his mouthpiece. He had let his thick black hair grow recently almost down to his shoulders (the teacher-training college had complained). Nia and her doll were paused en route around the room, looking at him; Helen knew she was surprised that her daddy hadn't greeted her with his usual exuberance.

—All day, Helen said, —I have to stop the children running around, in case the Underwoods start banging on the ceiling.

—Let them bang. We pay our rent, we have a perfect right for our children to run around, for me to practise my music if I want to.

—Don't raise your voice, she said. —They'll hear you.

—What the hell do I care, if they hear me?

—I have to live here with them, all day every day.

—Then let's move. This is insane. I need to play. We need to feel free, in our own home.

—We'll never find a flat as nice as this, in such a nice area, for this rent.

—What do I care about nice?

—I care.

—I can't live like this, Phil shouted. —You're killing me. He dropped the alto on the couch and rolled on to the floor, shouting at whoever might be listening in the flat below as loud as he could, with his face down against the carpet. —You're bloody killing me! For Christ's sake!

Helen threw the scrubbing brush hard at him. Dirty water sprayed around; the brush bounced against his temple, wooden side down, and he yelped in real pain and surprise. —Jesus Christ! Nia looked astonished and embarrassed. Helen went into the bedroom and closed the door behind her and lay down on the bed. Sophie was still asleep in her cot in the corner, her breathing weightless and tiny as a feather on the air. The rank smell of Phil's hair on the pillow filled Helen's nose and senses; her heart seemed to be leaping to escape out of her breast. They quite often quarrelled; what she said to herself usually was that Phil was like a child, emotional and volatile. But today she believed it when he said she was killing him. She had been washing the floor so contentedly, and then in the space of a few minutes her body had been seized and occupied by this violent tempest; she saw starkly that their two lives now were set against one another, that he was desperate for freedom and art and that she needed to stop him having them. She had heard the scrubbing brush crack against his skull; she couldn't pretend that it wasn't true, that she didn't want to destroy him. It was horrible, that they were yoked together in this marriage. She thought that if they went on like this she might one day soon tear his saxophone out of his mouth and stamp on it and break its keys.

When Phil went out to play that evening Helen packed a suitcase and a bag and caught a bus with the children to go to where her mother lived about three miles away across the city. She could only carry enough for one night; she even left behind the pushchair, which was too heavy and too difficult to fold down. She didn't mean, though, ever to go back to Phil. She had no idea of what lay ahead in the future, although she did think that if only she could get back her old job at the dance school, then perhaps her mother would look after the children while she worked. This wasn't likely, however, as the management at the dance school had changed and she didn't know the new people. She and Phil had eaten the tea she cooked in silence; they hadn't said goodbye when he went out. Helen had thought, as she always thought when he left to play, that he might be killed that night and she might never see him again: he would be driving home when he was tired and had been drinking, on unknown roads in the dark. She always pictured these roads as twisting through forest or bleak moorland, shining and treacherous with wet. But even then she didn't run after him. The clamour of his footsteps on the staircase died away. She heard him open the garage door and drive out the car, then stop and get out and close the garage door behind him. Then he drove off.

The clouds that had muffled the day like a fleece broke up in the evening and floated as pink wisps in a high sunny sky; a thrush was joyous in the garden as they left. Helen had Sophie on her leading rein, and could just manage the suitcase as long as she would walk. She didn't care if the Underwoods saw her go. The little girls loved catching buses. They had to get one down to the centre and then change; Helen was only afraid that as it got past Sophie's bedtime she would grumble and rub her eyes and want to be picked up. But the girls seemed to understand that this evening didn't exist inside the envelope of ordinary time; they cast quick buoyant wary looks at their mother, as if they mustn't make too much of anything. Nia, who had seen Helen throw the brush, practised an air of easy adaptation. Sophie held on to the chrome rail of the seat in front and bounced. When Helen clenched her fist on the rail, so that if the bus stopped suddenly and Sophie flew forwards she wouldn't hit her face, she was surprised to see she was still wearing her engagement and wedding rings, distorting lumps under her glove. All that seemed left already far behind.

Helen's father had died three years before; her mother had sold the big house where she had lived for thirty-five years and gone to live above a hairdresser's. Socially, she had come down in the world. Her husband had been retail manager for one of the big department stores; she had used to come to this hairdresser's as a customer, to have her hair washed and set, preserving a proper dignified distance from the staff. Now she even worked as a receptionist for them several afternoons a week, drawn deeply and happily into the world of their gossip and concerns. The only entrance to her flat was through the hairdresser's; Helen had to ring the doorbell, then her mother peered down from between her sitting-room curtains to see whoever was calling at this time. She didn't have a telephone, so Helen hadn't been able to warn her. A few minutes later they could see her feeling her way along the row of dryers in the dim light from the stairs behind; she didn't like to use the salon lights because they weren't on her bill. No one knew that Nia's dreams were visited by dryer-monsters with blank skin faces and huge bald egg-shaped skulls in powder blue. The glass door to the salon, hung inside with a rattling pink venetian blind, had 'Jennifer's' stencilled across it in flowing cursive script, and underneath that a pink silhouette bust of a lady in an eighteenth-century wig.

Helen and her mother weren't very alike. Everything about Helen had always been poised and quiveringly defiant; her mother seemed in contrast compliant and yielding. They didn't look alike: Helen had her father's stark cheekbones and strong colouring, her mother had been pinkly pretty and had faded and grown plump. But Helen was aware of a stubbornness deep down in her mother's softness; when you pushed, she didn't give way. When Helen was a teenager she and her mother had fought over every single thing –

over dancing, over make-up, over Phil – as if one of them must destroy the other before it could end; Helen's father, who had always appeared to be the stern parent, could only look on in perplexity. It was through the birth of the babies that they had been reconciled; as if that blood sacrifice had satisfied both their honours. Now, as soon as she had undone the bolts and opened the salon door, Nana Allen seemed to know intuitively what had happened.

—You've left him, she said. —He didn't hit you, did he? Has he been drinking?

Helen gave a little bleat of laughter and pressed the back of her wrist against her mouth. —I hit him. I threw something at him and hit him on the side of the head.

—A scrubbing brush, explained Nia solemnly.

Nana Allen laughed then too.

—Oh God, these children saw it, Helen said; and then for the first time tears spilled out from her eyes and ran down her cheeks.

—Sophie didn't see it, Nia corrected.

—Get them inside, her Nana said. —Come on in, my little lambs. Come and get warm in Nana's flat. Have you eaten anything? I've got some casserole.

Nia got past the egghead dryers by clinging on to her nana's skirt and burying her eyes in the familiar comfortable-smelling cloth. Helen couldn't believe these tears, now that they came; they hadn't been part of how she had imagined her exit, or her austere altered life. She hadn't even known she had inside her whatever deep reservoir of sorrow the tears poured from, flooding out of her, wave after wave, so that she was sodden, sobbing, helpless to speak. Her mother made her sit down in the corner of the sofa, wrapping her up in the old wartime quilt from home that she put over her knees in the evenings against the draughts (before Helen came she had been sitting reading her library book). She made cups of milky sweet tea for the children, made Nia a pickled-onion sandwich, gave them the biscuit barrel full of lemon creams; she had a special pronged fork for the pickled onions, with a pusher on a spring to press them off on to your plate. Helen eventually was able to drink a cup of tea too. The women together put the children to bed: Sophie in Nana's bed because it was wider and she was less likely to fall out of it, Nia in the bed in the spare room, which they had to make up first. They left the doors just open, in case the children called out. Then they sat and talked together for hours. Helen's mother held her hand while they talked, and stroked her hair, and brought a cool flannel for her to wipe her face. Nia could just hear their voices, although she couldn't hear the words. She fell asleep and the voices became a kind of loose safety net into which she fell, drooping and stretching under her, bearing her up, letting her go.

—I hate him, Helen said adamantly at some point that evening. —He hates me. We're killing each other. It's horrible. But I've seen through the whole thing, now. I couldn't ever put myself back inside it.

She was pacing about the room then with her old important restlessness, that still irritated her mother sometimes. She stopped to light another cigarette; the ashtray was already full, they were both smoking. Helen sucked on the cigarettes as if she was drinking the smoke down thirstily.

—Love is such a lie, she said. —In marriage, it's a lie. You kiss each other goodbye in the morning but actually inside you're both burning up with anger at things the other one's done or not done, and relief at getting rid of them for a few hours. I don't love him any more. I see right through him. All he cares about is his music and actually I agree with him: why shouldn't he?

—You gave up your dancing.

Helen looked at her in surprise. —I wasn't very good.

146

Not good enough. I wouldn't want Phil to give up his music. That's not the point.

—I thought you were very good.

(In fact she had exerted her utmost powers to dissuade Helen from a career in dance.)

—All those jazz standards about love and women, Helen went on, indifferent for the moment to the long-ago story of her dancing. —But actually they're only interested in each other, they're not genuinely interested in women at all. I mean, not once they've got what they want. All they're thinking about when they play all those songs about the women they can't bear to live without, the beautiful women they've lost, is actually what other men think. Am I playing it as well as him? What does he think of the way I did that solo? Is he impressed?

—He does care about you.

—No, he doesn't. He thinks I'm his enemy. He wants to be free.

—It will seem different tomorrow morning.

—It won't. Or if it does, then it won't be the truth. I will be lying to myself again.

Nia woke up very early. She knew at once where she was, from the way a vague light was swelling behind her nana's lilac-coloured silky curtains. Even though Nia didn't go to school yet – she only went three afternoons a week to a little nursery where in fine weather they lay on mats in the playground to nap – that lilac-toned light already meant to her a precious freedom from routine. Usually the accompaniment to the lilac light at Nana's was the sound of car engines starting up in the street outside and then droning deliciously away into the distance; but it was too early even for that to have begun.

Helen was in the bed with her. She had forgotten to wonder where her mother would sleep. Once or twice at home Nia had been put into bed with her when she was ill, but it was a rare, strange treat. Helen had her back turned and her head buried down in the pillows. She was wearing her blue seersucker pyjamas, and snoring slightly; she smelled of cigarettes. Her hair still had some of its backcombed stiffness from the day, only matted and flattened; Nia reached out her fingers and felt it sticky with hairspray. She lifted herself carefully on one elbow, to survey her mother from this unaccustomed advantage of consciousness; everyone was asleep in the flat apart from her. Helen hadn't taken her make-up off before she came to bed: some of it was smeared on Nana's pillowcase. She radiated heat, and gave off her usual beloved complicated smell, like face powder and fruit cake. Shut up and inactive behind her closed eyes, frowning in her sleep, she seemed more and not less mysterious. Nia settled down again, pressing up cautiously behind her mother so as not to wake her. Through the puckery material of the pyjamas she could feel against her face the skin of her mother's warm back; she breathed in and out with her mouth open, tasting her. She wondered if their lives had changed, and if she would be able to sleep with her mother every night from now on. Anything seemed possible.

Some time later she was wakened again by a sound of knocking, then of Jennifer (who wasn't really Jennifer but Patsy) opening the salon door and speaking crossly to someone with a man's voice: her daddy. Then the doorbell rang up in the flat. Helen sat bolt upright in bed, as though she came from sleep to full consciousness in one movement; she slithered her legs over the side of the bed and dashed into the sitting room, where she collided with Phil who had just dashed upstairs. She gave out a little moan: of subsidence, remorse, relief. Nia snuggled into the warm space her mother left behind. She could hear Jennifer moving about downstairs, tidying up and running water. She knew that soon the bell on the salon door would begin to tinkle as the staff arrived, and then the customers. If she was lucky she would be allowed down later. The hairdryers were only harmless and comical during the day; she would sit out of the way and play with the perm papers.

Forty years later, only Nia can remember any of this. Sophie was too young to remember. Nana Allen is long dead; and Nia's father is dead too, in his fifties, of a heart attack. When Nia tells the story to her mother, Helen simply flatly denies it; and Nia is sure she isn't pretending, that she's genuinely forgotten. In her late sixties Helen is still elegant and striking-looking, with suffering deep-set eyes and beautiful skin ('Never use soap on your face, Nia'). She complains about her hairdresser, but he's good: she has her hair dyed a dark honey colour with silver streaks, cut to fall loose and straight in a boyish look she calls 'gamine'. People who meet Helen think she must have been something impor-tant, a broadcaster or a designer, although actually what she has mostly done in her life is that old-fashioned thing: being an attractive and interesting woman. She has had two signif-icant relationships with men since Phil died, but she wouldn't marry either of them, although (she says, and Nia believes) they begged her. One of these men died too, and the other went back to his wife. The way she tells it now, the relationship with Phil Cerruti was the true love of her life, because Phil was a true artist. Nia isn't meaning to challenge this, either, when she brings up the subject of the time they ran away to Nana Allen's.

—I won't deny we did fight, Helen says. —We were both pretty passionate people. But no, I would remember it if I'd ever actually left him. I don't think the possibility would have crossed my mind. By the standards of today, of course I should have left. Everything in our family life had to be fitted around his music; you can't domesticate a real musician. But I was happy. The women of your generation wouldn't stand for it, darling, I know. But we'd been brought up to believe you stuck by your husband and that was it. You took the rough with the smooth.

On the other hand, Helen does now sometimes talk about her dancing. It has become part of her story, that she could have had a career as a dancer and she gave it up because that's how it was in those days, if you married and had children; the way she tells it, you can't tell whether she thinks the sacrifice was a shame or a splendid thing. Helen and Nia get on reasonably well most of the time these days. When Nia was in her twenties she went through (as she sees it now) a drearily dogmatic feminist phase. She lived for a while as a lesbian, and camped at Greenham Common. She gave herself a new name because she didn't want to use her father's, and then when Phil died (suddenly, so that she never said goodbye to him) she went into a depression for two years, and only came out of it with the help of therapy. Now she works as a therapist herself, and has a steady relationship with a man, Paul, although they don't live together and don't have any children. (Sophie has two boys and a girl, so Helen isn't cheated of grandchildren.)

Nia suggested to her mother last Christmas that in the spring the two of them should fly together to New York, to see the exhibition of Rubens drawings at the Met. The teacher at Helen's art classes had said how wonderful they were; and Helen had never been to America. It should have been one of those brilliant late-night inspirations that crumble to nothing in the light of practicalities, but somehow they really went ahead with this and booked their flights and their hotel. Then it was too late to change their minds, although in the week before they left Nia was consumed with doubt and dismay, imagining every kind of disaster. Her mother who suffered from angina wouldn't be able to walk anywhere; she would be taken ill, and Nia would have to deal with the American medical system. Or they would quarrel over something and not be able to escape from one another. On the flight over, Nia sat in the window seat and looked down at the unpopulated earth below, wherever it was, Greenland or Canada: for hundreds of miles, nothing but the black whorls and coils of rock, snow and winding rivers and frozen lakes. There was no cloud layer; there must be unbroken cold sunshine down there. She calmed herself by imagining she was translated down into that landscape; though not of course in her hopeless human body, which would only know how to stumble around in it and die.

They arrived in New York in torrential rain. The hotel in Greenwich Village, where Nia had stayed once before with Paul, looked rougher than she remembered. It was the kind of place she and Paul enjoyed, full of atmosphere and the traces of an older New York which they knew from films, with a marble-faced dado and huge gilt mirrors in the hallway, little metal mailboxes for the permanent residents, a lift painted around inside with acanthus blooms, oddly assorted books on the shelves in every room. Now she could only see it through her mother's eyes. The furniture was cheap, made from split cane. They had to use a bathroom out on the corridor, and the first time Nia went in there she found a dirty sticking plaster on the floor. The breakfasts were awful, in a basement where a fierce Hispanic woman presided over Thermoses full of coffee and hot water. Mother and daughter were both shy, transplanted out of the worlds they knew. Nia was often anxious, worrying about how to get from place to place, and where to eat, and whether Helen was tired; probably Helen was worrying too.

They were also always aware, however, that they would think about the things they were doing as wonders, afterwards, when they got home. Their shared bedroom had a view on to the street of elegant and wealthy brownstones, where the trees were just coming into leaf. While Helen did her face and hair at the dressing table in the mornings, Nia (who only showered and towelled her short hair dry) watched out of the window, exclaiming at the New York dogs: extravagantly big or small or pampered, sometimes being exercised in gangs of five or six by bored professional walkers. They gave up the hotel basement and found a place round the corner which did breakfasts of rough peasant bread and seed bread with real fruit jam and *café au lait* in bowls; they made friends with the waiter. And on their second day the sun came out and was even hot; they took a boat trip to the Statue of Liberty and the Immigration Museum on Ellis Island; they marvelled at the Manhattan skyline. Helen persuaded Nia to let her pay for some oatmeal cotton trousers and a long moss-green cardigan; Nia in the expensive Fifth Avenue shops felt cornered and oversized and fraudulent. She longed for the new clothes to trans-form her, to prove that her mother's old instincts hadn't lapsed or fallen out of date.

After they had seen the Rubens drawings they had tea in the American Wing café in the Met, and watched through the glass wall a gang of workers in Central Park, pulling the ivy out of the bare winter trees. They tied ropes around it and heaved together until the ivy came away in heavy masses, which the men then fed on a conveyor belt into a shredder. Helen that day was wearing a grey suit and a silk scarf decorated with blue and yellow birds; the scarf had got somehow skewed sideways so that it stuck up rakishly behind one ear and made her look as if she was drunk or slightly dotty. Nia could see, too, where her lipstick was bleeding into the fine wrinkles at the edges of her lips. She talked about the mistakes Sophie was making with her chil-dren, in a tone of tactful light regret which Nia knew Sophie found particularly maddening. After tea when Helen came out from the Ladies, where she would have checked herself in the mirror, the scarf was tidied into its usual casual elegance. She looked tired, though, and had to use her angina spray when they were walking from the museum to find a taxi.

—Don't those exquisite drawings simply make everything worthwhile? she said when they were back in their hotel room, groaning and easing her feet out of her shoes.

—Are you all right? Nia stood over her, surly because she was worried.

—Don't fuss, said Helen. —I'm an old woman.

She undressed down to her petticoat, so as not to rumple her suit, and lay on her back on her twin bed, her head propped on the pillows in the careful way Nia recognised as protecting her hairdo. The room was bright with evening sunshine. They had made its seediness homely with their clothes hung about, their scarves and beads and books mingled together, their flannels and bottles and sponge bags on the sink.

—Where would you like to go to eat tonight?

Helen sighed. —I'm so comfortable here.

—We don't have to go out, said Nia, full of doubt. —But won't you get hungry?

—I'm not worried about me. But what about you, darling? You'll need something.

Nia went to find the delicatessen they had noticed a few blocks away, to buy food they could eat in their room. It was the first time she had been out alone, and it was a relief to be able to use her long stride instead of continually adjusting her pace to her mother's. She felt as if she was really part of New York at last, choosing cold meat and bread and olives, and fruit juice. She bought yogurts, too, forgetting that they didn't have spoons; it was Helen who suggested that they could scoop these up with the wrong ends of their toothbrushes. While they ate their picnic they became deeply involved in a real-life courtoom drama on the television, debating it passionately. When that was finished they undressed and climbed under the bedcovers and fell asleep, even though it was very early.

Some time in the night Nia half woke and was confused, not knowing where she was. Outside on the street a car started up, and then the drone of its engine faded into the distance. She lifted her head off her pillow in the incomplete dark, and knew from the smell of face powder and cake and the light snoring that her mother was somewhere close by. She seemed to feel the radiation of her heat; and she remembered the seersucker pyjamas, dotted with little blue rosebuds.

—I'm still here, Nia thought, reassured and happy, falling back easily into her sleep. —She's still here.